Darkwalker

The Sunwalker Trilogy Book 3

S. T. SANCHEZ

ISBN 978-0-999001-66-0

thepamperedcatpress.com

Also by S. T. SANCHEZ

The Keeper Archives

The Portal Keeper
The Secret of the Realms
The Keeper's Batallion

The Sunwalker Trilogy

Sunwalker

Nightwalker

Darkwalker

For Dawn,

Who continues to support me by reading my drafts before they go to my editor. Which is a scary and daunting challenge.

&

For **Red,**

You'll be missed. Hopefully someday you will forgive me for killing you off in book two. R.I.P.

Chapter I

CURSED

"No!" Tread gasped, horrified, as he dropped the note to the floor. "He's going to turn her into a darkwalker."

"He wouldn't," Alex said, covering her mouth with her hand as she turned to Vanessa.

"Actually, that sounds like exactly the sort of thing my brother would come up with," the eight-hundred-year-old vampire replied.

"What is a darkwalker?" Lilly asked, wanting to be clued in. She had heard Tread mention the term before, but had let it go. Now she shuddered, unsure if she really wanted to know.

Lilly watched as Tread stood numbly in front of her. The note lying on the cold tile floor. Lilly snatched it, quickly reading it, unable to believe the words she had heard. It was as if the world had stopped spinning. Nothing mattered anymore. Nothing but retrieving her mother.

To whom it may concern:

Something invaluable of mine was taken. So, I think it's only fair to respond in kind. I will have to live with the pain you have caused me for eternity, and while death is the ultimate punishment for some, I believe it would be too generous for you.

My army of nightwalkers will soon rule this world and I will reign in paradise. I don't foresee a place for you in it. However, until that day I will content myself with finding bits of happiness where I can. Elaine will prove to be most entertaining, of that, I am certain. Until then I bid you adieu. I hope to see you soon. However, not all of you have the same amount of time left, so you may want to hurry. Tick tock.
Cheers,
KOYT
P.S. I hope Elaine's not afraid of the <u>*DARK*</u>

The scent of blood wafted up from the letter. Although it had dried, Lilly could tell it was still fresh. For the first time she wondered if there was a God and offered up her first silent prayer. She prayed that this *ink* hadn't come from her mother, but held out little hope. A sickening feeling formed in the pit of her stomach, and all she could see was red.

Koyt, Tread's former best friend, his dead sister's mate, had come to their community, Spero, waving a white flag of truce. And Lilly had stupidly let him in. True, the blame could be pointed at others too, but if Lilly had just sent him packing the moment he had showed his face, she wondered if this could have all been avoided.

Probably not. He was a sunwalker with several hundred years on her. Torturing her father, Dylan, for seventeen years hadn't been enough revenge. No, he had to come here and try to kill Tread, his ex-friend. The vampire he blamed for betraying Sage's memory, although Lilly's father and other VAS officers had committed the actual murder. This vendetta all began when Tread released his twin sister's killer, Dylan. Koyt couldn't let it go. He would have murdered Tread if Vanessa, Tread's adoptive mother, and Koyt's own sister, hadn't come and saved him.

Dragon steel had been their only surviving grace. If Vanessa hadn't been wielding a sword edged with the rare metal, things would have ended far worse for the town of Spero. Tread for one would not be standing here now.

Now the fiend had struck another incapacitating blow, one far worse than Lilly could have imagined. While she had been preoccupied with trying to save Tread and making sure her father was safe, he had snuck by them yet again, kidnapping her mother, Elaine.

Underestimating him had been her downfall. She would never let that happen again. After reading the note again, Lilly was still confused. She could tell Koyt was taunting them, but she felt like she was missing something.

Lilly glanced around the room. "What is a darkwalker?" she asked again, shifting her eyes around at her fellow vampires, then focusing on Tread. That is what Tread had said Koyt was going to turn Elaine into. Something Alex couldn't quite believe.

He was muttering to himself and seemed to be in another place.

"It's a vampire..." Alex, Tread's friend from Little Rock, began looking uncertain, "...a different kind...something happens to them when they go through the transformation." She looked apologetically at Lilly. "They don't turn out right." Alex turned to Vanessa. "Can they really be made? I thought it just happened sometimes, and that no one knew why. Something to do with bad genes, maybe."

Vanessa opened her mouth but was interrupted before she could begin.

"They are created." Tread sighed.

Lilly turned back to face him. "How?" she asked.

It seemed to physically pain him as he spoke the words. "The same rules apply to creating a darkwalker as a regular vampire. They have to be bitten. Venom has to be injected, and they must consume human blood prior to the transformation," he paused, looking at her guiltily, "but with one key exception. Darkwalkers can only be created if they turn during a full moon."

"Why?" Alex and Lilly asked at the same time.

It was hard to not want to hold Tread completely responsible for this nightmare she was living. After all, Tread had let Koyt stay. Dismissed every doubt and concern Lilly had voiced.

"Beats me." He shrugged. "I've heard rumors, some are sheer nonsense. Nothing really makes any sense. Some say because most vampires are creatures of the night and a full moon is the one night a month that provides the most light...well, that it does something to the vampire. Vampires should be created in darkness. Darkness protects them." He shook his head. "I've heard it's a curse. That centuries ago a witch fell in love with a vampire and was betrayed. The vampire fell in love with a human, and on the night of a full moon, tried to gift his love with immortality. The scorned witch cursed the other woman, and that's where darkwalkers came from."

He looked to Vanessa for confirmation. "I don't know about you, but I've never met any witches in my entire existence."

"Not that I've come across," Vanessa agreed.

"There are a few other stories I've heard. They all sound equally far-fetched. But it doesn't matter." Tread pushed his hair out of his face. "How darkwalkers came to be isn't important. What's imperative is that they do exist." He turned and faced Lilly, a look of determination in his eyes. "We can't let that happen to your mother."

"But what makes them different from Alex or Henry or any of the many nightwalkers that live here in Spero? So, they are created under the light of a full moon—what does it do to them that causes them to become a darkwalker?" Lilly asked, frustrated that the answers were not coming quickly enough. Her mother was out there in the hands of a psychopath. Why was it so difficult for them to understand the urgency of her understanding the situation?

Tread shook his head solemnly. "The short answer? It makes them crazy—raving mad—no one can reason with them." He rubbed his face, looking emotionally exhausted. "The longer answer…Well, I've never met one, but I've heard stories from vampires who have. It's like some wires get twisted inside their brain during the transformation. Whoever they loved or desired most during their human existence becomes their fixation. They become crazed with a feeling that nothing will be right until that one person who mattered most to them is dead. Apparently, the only thing that ends the lunacy is when the darkwalker has drained their loved one completely. I've heard they won't kill anyone else until their obsession is dead."

Lilly gasped, covering her mouth with her hand and shuddering. "That's horrible. We can't allow my mother to become one of those things." She shook her head, then looked up with a shred of hope in her eyes. "Do you think the rumors could be wrong? I mean, you've never met one." Lilly grabbed at Tread's shirt, desperate for reassurance. "Maybe the stories have been exaggerated."

Vanessa stepped forward and placed her hand gently on Lilly's shoulder. "They haven't, child," she said sullenly.

Lilly released Tread from her grip as all eyes turned to Vanessa. "I've encountered two in my existence," she began. "When we hear of one, we act quickly to terminate them. Or we did before humans became aware of our existence. No one wanted attention drawn to our kind."

"Who's we?" Alex asked, clearly surprised.

It made Lilly feel slightly better that she wasn't the only vampire that appeared to not know the entire history of their kind.

"Just older vampires. Those who've been around long enough to know that less is more. The less knowledge humans have about us, the better it is for our kind."

"But if they only kill the object of their obsession, why bother with hunting them down?" Alex wondered.

"Darkwalkers can still draw outside attention rather quickly. Imagine a crazy human. They stand out because they act different. But an insane vampire, going at vamp speed, tearing apart cities, trying to find one individual…" Vanessa shrugged, not finishing the sentence.

"So, what happened in the two cases you witnessed?" Tread asked.

Vanessa breathed out slowly. "The first we beheaded immediately. It was clear that none of us could reason with the darkwalker. They can't be talked out of it, even knowing death is imminent. It was over in a minute." She snapped her fingers. "The second was different. I was with a friend when we found the darkwalker. I convinced him to help me capture it. We imprisoned the poor soul." She looked tired and older than normal as she spoke of the past. "We found the vampire who had created it. Her name was Rebecca. She told us the creature had a sister. So as an experiment, we tracked down the sister and brought her to the darkwalker. The darkwalker became frenzied at the sight of her. The sister tried to reason with her, but it was the same. There was no sign of anything but a monster; not even a hint of humanity remained. Eventually, in a desire to learn more, we put the sister in the cage with the darkwalker. It was over quickly. The sister was devoured in seconds."

Lilly gasped loudly.

Vanessa nodded, "It was a terrible thing to do," she acknowledged. "But we needed information. We felt that one human life was worth the risk if we could figure out how to stop or end the craze. And then as soon as the sister was dead, the darkwalker changed. It was as if she transformed into a normal vampire." Vanessa shook her head. "Upon realizing who she had killed, the vampire couldn't live with herself. Grief overcame her and she committed suicide by vamp."

"Suicide by what?" Lilly asked, confused.

"Have you ever heard of suicide by cop? In the movies, when a perp doesn't want to go on but can't live with their actions, they attack a cop, or do something that forces the officer to kill them. Suicide by police," Tread explained.

Vanessa nodded in agreement. "She attacked my friend, and forced me to end her existence. I watched it all. I am certain that she couldn't deal with the blood on her hands."

"No, no, no, no," Lilly said, more to herself, shaking her head. "This can't be happening." No wonder the vampire wanted to end her existence. What she did would be impossible for anyone to get over. But after hearing the story, Lilly didn't think the blood was only on the darkwalker's hands. Vanessa and her friend had proven themselves to be equally guilty—probably more so than the murderer—in Lilly's mind. The darkwalker had been out of her mind, not realizing what she was doing. Vanessa had no such excuse.

Tread walked over to try to comfort her, but she held up her hand to stop him. She needed a moment. Looking around the apartment, it was hard to believe how much had changed. She looked at the stove in the kitchen. She could picture her mother standing at it, flipping pancakes and making scrambled eggs, her father's favorite. She moved to the kitchen table. They had spent hours playing scrabble together. It was her mother's favorite game. Some of the letters had been lost so Tread had carved new ones out of wood. Next she looked at the sofa where her mother would curl up and read a book when she had the chance.

Everything in their apartment reminded her of Elaine. Memories flooded her mind. She had to get her mother back. She needed her.

Lilly took a deep breath. "So, when is the next full moon? If he is going to do this, then he has to wait for that, correct?"

Vanessa nodded.

"In twenty-five days," Alex answered solemnly.

Koyt could be anywhere in the world and Lilly only had less than a month to find him, kill him, and rescue her mother before he turned Elaine into a monster.

Chapter II

BLOCKED

"Okay. So where are they? Where did Gavin and the rest of Koyt's goons end up?" Lilly glanced around. "The jail, right?"

After Koyt entered the community, he convinced several of their residents to join his side. Gavin, Terri, Chloe, and Matthew were four of the vampires Lilly knew had sided with Koyt, along with his pal Hunter who had accompanied him when they first arrived. Who knew if there were any others that they hadn't discovered? Lilly hoped not, but Koyt always seemed to have the upper hand and had accomplished more than any of them imagined possible.

Tread shook his head uncertainly.

Then Lilly remembered he had been a little preoccupied with trying to keep his head attached to pay much attention to anything else that had happened immediately after his scuffle with Koyt.

"They have to be there," Lilly insisted. It was the only place that made sense. "Tread, you can torture the information out of them—you've had plenty of practice."

Tread's mouth dropped open, looking horrified by her suggestion and comment. Alex stared at her wide-eyed.

Lilly paused for a moment. "Sorry. I didn't mean it like that. I'm just…"

"Terrified," Vanessa suggested, supplying the word. She patted Lilly consolingly on the back. "We understand. Take me to them and I'll get the information out of them."

"Whoa! Hold on a minute. We can't just go torturing people," Tread said, waving his hands in front of him and barring Vanessa's path.

"Sure we can," Lilly said, brushing him off. "They took my mother." She glanced at Vanessa and motioned for her to follow.

"No, we can't," Tread insisted, grabbing Lilly's arm.

Lilly glared at Tread. "LET. GO. OF. ME." Her words were slow and deliberate.

"Not until we discuss this," Tread responded, loosening his grip a little. "Lil, this isn't you. We can't just torture them. Koyt took your mom. We don't even know if they knew anything about that or not. AND—" he barreled through, seeing Lilly try to interrupt, "we are not a dictatorship. You have made that clear. You need to convene the council. You can't just make rules as you see fit, no matter how justified you feel."

The room fell silent waiting to see how Lilly would react. Alex took a step back, uncertain of the emotions flying around the room.

Lilly let out a long sigh. It infuriated her that Tread was right. That now, after all the things he had done in his past, he was the one pushing her to make the moral choice. A small part of her wished he could just flip a switch and turn back into the vampire who didn't value life. The one who might have even relished in the act of torturing another being. But Lilly knew that wasn't fair. "All right. I'm listening."

He hesitantly released his grip on her.

"I will try to be more rational. But let's wake the council now. I don't want to delay. Every second that passes, Koyt is doing who knows what to my mother. And I'm not taking torture off the table."

"I really doubt that after tonight anyone is sleeping," Vanessa guessed.

Still unsure of Lilly's state of mind, Tread looked to Alex. "Will you make sure Lilly goes straight to Town Hall?"

Alex nodded; Lilly rolled her eyes.

Why did I ever give her a tour?

"Vanessa can come with me. We will round everyone up." Tread motioned to the door with his head and his adopted mother followed him outside.

It didn't take long for Tread to track everyone down. Mark and Annie had been together at the clinic. Lex was home but awake, horrified to find out Elaine had been taken. It took some coaxing on both Tread's and Vanessa's part to get Ethan to even allow his wife to attend the meeting after the events of the last few hours. Justin had been lifting weights. Ellen's place still hadn't been filled. The vote was supposed to take place tomorrow, but Tread doubted that would happen now.

Looking around the room, it didn't escape Lilly that Vanessa wasn't here. True, she was not a member of the council, but Lilly felt certain that Tread had sent her away solely due to the fact that Vanessa was not opposed to torture. Lilly didn't even wait until everyone was seated before she began.

"As I am sure you have all been informed by now, my mother Elaine has been abducted."

Lex looked empathetically at her friend as the others all slowly nodded in affirmation.

"We're so sorry," Annie said.

"Yes, your mother was nice from what I could tell. I mean, she didn't hate vampires," Mark agreed.

"I appreciate the sentiment, but that's not going to help me find her," Lilly began. "Gavin, Chloe, Matthew, Terri, and Hunter are all confined to cells in the prison." She had confirmed this with Annie before the meeting commenced. Knowing they were a few short minutes from her location was really testing her self-control.

Rationally, she knew Tread was right. Torture was wrong. But all she wanted to do was pull them each apart limb by limb until she found her mother. Right or wrong, Lilly would do whatever she had to if it brought Elaine back. The consequences could be dealt with later.

"We need to interrogate them and decide how far we are willing to go."

"How far?" Justin asked. "So are we talking executions, banishment, or more along the lines of…waterboarding?" He looked around uncertainly at the other council members.

"Whatever it takes," Lilly answered, determination shining in her eyes. Although waterboarding was pointless, as vampires didn't need oxygen to survive.

Lex looked to Annie, not wanting to meet her friend's eyes. "I always heard torture doesn't work. That people will just tell you what they think you want to hear to get the pain to stop. Do we know that they have information on Koyt's whereabouts?"

"No, we don't," Tread interjected firmly before Lilly could answer.

"Well, I don't feel comfortable voting to torture information out of someone that may not even have the intel we need to begin with," Lex answered sheepishly.

"This is my mom we are talking about here Lex!" Lilly yelled. "She would do anything for you."

Her friend shrunk down in the chair as her eyes began to water.

Justin stood up and put his hand on Lex's shoulder consolingly. "I agree with Lex. I'm sorry, Lilly. I am not opposed to prison sentences or even executions since they essentially betrayed out community, but torture feels like something Koyt would do. It's not us." Then he glanced down at Lex who was dabbing her tears with a sleeve. "We're all your friends here. Let's not forget that."

"I feel the same," Mark agreed. "Let's negotiate sentencing and see what we can come up with. Offer a deal to the first one who talks."

"Agreed," Annie assented. "And I don't think you," she turned to Lilly, "should be in there during the interrogations. You are too close to this."

Lilly balked and stormed out of the council room.

Lex got up and followed her out into the hallway.

"Mark, want to come do some interrogating with me?" Tread asked, hopeful.

"Sure."

Lilly paced the hallway angrily. She needed to calm down, but her fury and anger just wouldn't subside.

She heard Lex before she saw her. Lilly knew her friend's footsteps, her breathing, even her smell.

"I'm sorry, Lilly."

She wanted to be angry at her friend. It felt like a betrayal to have her BFF side against her. But knowing Lex had cancer and not knowing how much time she had left…Lilly didn't want to waste it fighting. Guilt was already swelling inside of her for making Lex cry.

"I don't want to argue. I know you've gotten your share of bad news today too. Let's just put this on the backburner for now and hope the good cop, bad cop routine works."

Lex looked up, surprised. "Bad news? What are you talking about?"

Of course she didn't know. When would Adam have had the time to tell Lex? Her uncle had just barely found out.

"I misspoke. It's been a long night," she lied, turning from her friend.

Lex reached forward and grabbed Lilly's arm. "Don't lie to me. We don't do that. We've never done that. Sometimes we disagree but we are always upfront about it." She slowly released her grip. "I know you. What bad news do I not know about?"

Lilly slowly spun back around. "I'm sorry, Lex. Adam should be the one to tell you this."

"Oh, so the Hib isn't gone. Well, I'll just take another dose of antibiotics. It's okay. I don't even feel that bad. I've just been a little tired and had a few nosebleeds."

"Oh Lex, if only it were Hib. I'm sorry, Uncle Adam says it's leukemia."

"No, he's wrong. I don't have cancer. I just need a little rest," Lex said, sounding more and more uncertain as she continued. She leaned against the wall and closed her eyes. After several minutes of silence, she finally spoke. "How am I going to tell Ethan? This will devastate him." She opened her eyes slowly, tears running down her cheeks.

Lilly stepped forward and hugged her friend. "I won't let anything happen to you. Ryan is going to figure something out. There are treatments."

Ryan Silver was the vice president's son. He had been abducted by Lord Steel and was a prisoner at the camp when Lilly had arrived. When she defeated the evil dictator, Lilly offered everyone the choice to stay or go. Ryan chose to leave. At the time, Lilly had no idea that Ryan was so well-connected with the government. Now she was so grateful.

Their relationship wasn't always smooth sailing. Lilly had been responsible for Ryan suffering in ways no one deserved. He had lost his arm because of her. Lilly had trusted the wrong vampire. Ryan hated her for it. But now that her mother had been taken, his heart seemed to soften. Probably because he now knew that Lilly would keep her word and would never stop until Koyt was dead. Ryan had saved their community once before by acquiring much needed medicine when an outbreak of Hib had hit Spero. Now she hoped he could produce another miracle. Lex's life depended on it.

"Don't tell Ethan." Lex sniffed, rubbing her eyes with her sleeve. "I'll tell him, but not yet. I want to wait to see what Ryan comes up with. He'll just worry too much if he knows now and that won't help anything."

"Of course. Whatever you need."

Lilly walked Lex home. That was one of the conditions to Ethan allowing his wife to attend the council meeting. She had to have a sunwalker escort. Tread was off hopefully interrogating vampires and getting answers, so that just left her.

As soon as her friend was safe inside, Lilly dashed over to the jail, praying that a substantial lead had been discovered.

"Koyt never told us anything," Lilly could hear Chloe whimpering. She took the steps down to the vampire cells in a single bound, landing lightly on the balls of her feet.

No one wanted Lilly anywhere near these interrogations. They were afraid—afraid of how she might be pushed over the edge and go too far, and perhaps they were right. But maybe, just maybe, to get the real answers, Koyt's goons needed to be afraid of someone.

Chloe was in the first cell. The door was cracked open and Mark and Tread were inside. Lilly could hear the hum of electricity running through the other cells, but this one had been deactivated for the moment.

Chloe glanced up and locked eyes with Lilly through the slit in the door. She scrambled off the stool and moved to the furthest corner of the room.

"I didn't know. I swear. He never mentioned taking your mother," she cried out, terrified.

Tread turned around, and Lilly could tell from the look on his face that he was less than pleased that she had come.

As if they could stop Lilly if she really wanted to end things. Mark was a weak nightwalker and although she felt ashamed for thinking it, Lilly knew Tread wouldn't be a problem either if it came to a fight. He was still recovering. Although he looked fine on the outside, his voice still sounded hoarse, and Lilly knew that with a little pressure in the right place she could incapacitate him for enough time if she really wanted to.

But as much as she wanted to tear Chloe limb from limb, that wouldn't get her answers.

Lilly stalked into the cell, daring Tread and Mark to try and stop her. "Why?" she demanded angrily. "Why betray us? What was so unbearable about the life we were building here?"

"Because I didn't want to die. Look what he did to Johnny." Her eyes shifted back and forth between Mark, Tread, and Lilly in a wild frenzy.

Johnny had been forced to steal blood from Spero. Koyt had set it up to distract them, to keep the attention away from himself. But by the time Lilly had figured it out, Koyt had Johnny killed. Anything to keep him from talking. Johnny only stole the blood in the first place because he thought Koyt would kill him. In the end, it wouldn't have mattered what choice he made. Koyt still murdered him, or had Hunter or one of his other goons do it.

"I'm sorry I'm not brave like you." Chloe's voice cracked from fear. "I don't have some moral high ground or a belief that good conquers evil. Koyt's ancient. There is no one, not even you Lilly, who can defeat him. So yeah, I did what he asked. I just wanted to live."

"You're pathetic," Lilly spit. She stepped closer, leaning her face a few centimeters away from Chloe's.

Out of the corner of her eye, Lilly could see Tread preparing himself to intervene if needed.

"Death isn't off the table yet," Lilly added icily, "so you better hope you can remember something worthwhile." She turned back to Mark. "Get her a pen and some paper," she barked harshly.

Mark dashed out of the room.

"Lil—"

"Who's next?" she demanded.

"No one." Tread blocked her path but didn't shrink back from the death stares he was receiving.

"We want to interview them each separately and there aren't enough cells to do that right now. Do you want us to put Chloe back in a cell with the others with her pen and paper?" he asked. "Because if she has anything to give us, I doubt she's going to write it down with the others in the cell."

Her mind flashed back to Johnny, decapitated and dead in his cell. "Who did you put in with Hunter?" she asked, but before waiting for an answer she rushed to the other two cells, peering in the small windows.

She breathed a sigh of relief when she saw that Hunter was alone and Matthew, Gavin, and Terri shared the other cell.

Tread arched his eyebrow and smiled her favorite smile, as if to let her know he had it covered. Lilly appreciated his quick thinking but couldn't let herself focus on anything but finding her mother at the moment.

She pushed past him and found Mark in the cell with Chloe. He stood to the side while she held a pen in one hand and a blank sheet of paper in the other.

"Mark, do you think you can handle Chloe on your own, upstairs?" Lilly pointed. "That way we can start *interviewing*," she used Tread's word, "the next *traitor*." He may have wanted to keep things more civil. But Lilly wanted no doubts in their minds as to what their new position was in Spero. It was the only leverage she had. Self-preservation was the strongest motivator most species had.

She moved swiftly and angrily to open the next cell, but Tread was faster, barring her path.

She could only imagine the look of fury on her face. She could see the hurt in his eyes just for a second, but he didn't back down.

"Out!" he commanded in a firm, harsh tone that Lilly had never heard before.

"No!" Lilly countered as she tried to push forward.

"Don't test me on this." He took a step forward and crossed his arms. "The council voted for you to sit this out. I can see the rage in your eyes. I know it. I've felt it." His face softened slightly. "Lil, I know I carry most of the blame in this. And you can hate me. But I won't let your rage consume you. I won't let you carry the same regrets I have. We will find your mother. I swear to you. But you will not enter that cell while I'm still standing. And I have a few years on you." He offered her a weak smile with his signature cocky eyebrow move, but it was half-hearted and she knew it.

She could see him tense, waiting for her next move. Her rage was all that was keeping her going. And she did hate Tread, but she hated herself too. When they did find her mother again, who did Lilly want to be? Someone Lilly couldn't stand to look at in the mirror? Or someone her mother would be proud of? Making the right choice didn't always mean things would be easier.

Nightmares of the lives she had taken still haunted her dreams.. It didn't matter how justified her actions seemed, it didn't make it any easier to stomach. But how could she handle having the blood of her own mother on her hands? It was all too much.

Lilly punched her fist into the wall of the prison and screamed, leaving a hole in the sheetrock. She looked once more at Tread, but knew if she hurt him, she would regret it once her mind cleared, and with that thought propelling her forward, she dashed out of the building.

She ran and didn't stop. When she got to the gate, she flew up the stairs and launched herself over the wall, startling Scott and Sam who were watching the northern gate, not wanting to pause for the time it would take them to open it.

Lilly didn't know how long she had run for, but fatigue was finally beginning to set in. Her rage had fueled her for the most part and was now a distant yet ever-present companion. But at least now it wasn't consuming her.

She looked around and saw an old road sign bent down so that the words weren't visible. She straightened it and even though some of the letters were missing and the sign had faded after so many years, she could tell she was somewhere in Arkansas. It hadn't seemed like she had covered that much distance.

A sudden breeze picked up blowing down from the north. Lilly crinkled her nose. Something smelled foul. After surveying the area, she spotted a run-down building off to the side of the road. The smell seemed to be coming from that direction.

It would have been condemned had it been in any of the big cities. The roof was half collapsed in, the windows were all shattered, whether by vandals from years ago or from just eroding over time, Lilly couldn't tell.

She headed toward the building and as she grew closer, she was certain her hunch had been right. Whatever was causing the stench was coming from inside.

The door, if you could call it that, was rotted and only appeared to be half intact. As Lilly pushed it open, a third of what had remained crumbled to the ground.

As she stepped over the debris, she entered what must have once been a restaurant. There were tables and chairs scattered around the room. Most were not in much better condition than the door. Brownish red streaks decorated the walls, and footprints had recently tread through the dust-ridden floors.

Someone had been here recently and a struggle had ensued. As she walked around a table, Lilly gasped. There was an arm sticking out from underneath one of the chairs, or what was left of one. Some wild animal had gnawed it down to almost nothing. What remained was scraps of rotted, decaying flesh.

The odor was overwhelming. It was times like these when her heightened sense of smell seemed a bit overrated. As Lilly stepped further into the dining area, she noticed there were more remnants of dead bodies. The pieces had been mauled too much, making it difficult to tell how many people had died here. It was enough to make Lilly sick, if that were possible.

In the far corner of the room, a flash of red caught her eye. As she turned her head Lilly realized it was hair. Then everything came together fast and hard. She felt as if she had been struck in the face. It should never have taken her this long to figure out. But she had been a little crazed as she ran here. Was it possible her subconscious had brought her here or had it been merely a coincidence?

This was where Koyt had met with Ryan and the senators. This was where her whole world began to crash down—where her suspicions of Koyt being the monster he was really solidified.

She was standing among the remains of the dead senators. And that flash of color that seemed so familiar was Red. She covered her mouth and stifled a sob. Slowly she made her way through the mess to the back corner of the room.

In the back of the building, Lilly saw the stairs that Ryan took to the roof. Her mind pieced together a picture of how she imagined the scene unfolding. Senators falling to the ground in quick succession, probably before they could even realize what was happening, Red coming to Ryan's defense because he knew Ryan was Lilly's friend. A brief but bloody struggle. And Ryan, hobbling up to the roof, collapsing in the chopper as Red paid the ultimate price for his loyalty to Lilly. Koyt would have made Red's death painful.

Because he was a vampire, Red was still preserved. His color had faded some but his body had not been ravaged by wild animals, whether because they could sense what he was, or if it was solely due to the fact that his body was nearly indestructible, she knew not.

The fault of Red's death rested with her and her alone. She had asked him to watch Koyt. He might not have intervened to save Ryan had she not petitioned him for his help. This was no place for his final resting spot, among the filth and stench.

A table cloth lay scattered a few feet behind her. Lilly picked it up and ran her fingers across the fabric. It was threadbare and felt weak and feeble. Uncertain it could take the weight of Red's body, she gathered two other cloths and laid them on top of each other, adding to their strength.

Carefully and reverently she placed first Red's head and then the rest of his pieces in the makeshift parcel. They were easy to find because of how well preserved they were, but he had been scattered throughout the building. Lilly didn't even want to try to imagine what Red must have suffered to end up in such a disarray. It would have been enough to decapitate him, but Koyt made sure he suffered in every way imaginable.

After carefully tying the table cloth securely closed, Lilly hefted the bag over her shoulder. She looked one last time at the bones and body parts, wondering which of the arms belonged to Ryan. She pushed the thought away and headed outside.

The senators deserved a proper burial as well. They had families and loved ones somewhere. When all of this was over, Lilly promised herself that she would return and make sure the other bodies were treated with the respect they deserved.

The fresh air was a welcome relief to her senses. Still unsure how secure her makeshift coffin was, Lilly started back towards Spero in a slow run. When she felt confident the sheets were holding, her pace increased, slowly at first, and then finally into her superhuman sprint.

The prisoners should have all had time to be interrogated by now. She wondered if Tread had gleaned anything useful. Koyt was too smart to give anyone his full plan. But perhaps he slipped up and one of his goons overheard something pertinent. Maybe they themselves didn't even realize it.

She hoped Tread would understand why she brought Red back. It was going to be a shock to see him like this at first, but Lilly hoped that being able to say goodbye and bury Red properly would bring him some peace.

More time must have passed than Lilly had thought because by the time she arrived back at the gate, Sam and Scott were no longer there. Annie waved down to her before opening the gate.

"I wasn't sure if we were going to see you again. You're lucky vampires can't have heart attacks because I am pretty sure Sam, Scott, or both of them would have had one from the way they tell of how fast you busted outta here." Annie arched her eyebrows curiously.

Lilly set her sack gingerly at her feet. "I just had to get out of here. I wasn't thinking straight. The run helped to clear my head and calm my nerves."

"I get it." Annie reached forward and patted Lilly's shoulder. "So," she began, changing the subject, "what's in the bag?"

"I'll tell you later," she promised. "First I need to find Tread."

She nodded in understanding. "I'd better get into the pathway anyway. Sun should be up soon."

It was already nearly morning. This night had been the shortest and longest of her life.

Chapter III

DECISIONS

U nsure of where to look for Tread, Lilly headed to the last place she had seen him. Mark was manning the desk inside the prison. Other than the sound of him shuffling his feet off the desk upon her entrance, she was greeted with silence.

That didn't necessarily mean Tread wasn't here. She knew there were others downstairs, none of which were stirring at the moment.

"Tread?" Lilly asked.

"Left a while ago." Mark shrugged. "Didn't say where he was headed."

"Did you get anything out of them?" Lilly asked.

"Not really. I don't think they were told much." He pulled open the desk's top drawer and retrieved a lined paper. He pushed it towards her. "Vanessa just dropped this off."

It was a list of places, Lilly realized as she scanned over it quickly. All the known residences of Vanessa's psychotic brother.

"Maybe this will jog one of their memories."

Whether Mark thought it was a good idea for Lilly to get involved or not, she wasn't sure. But she was glad that he made no attempt to stop her as she made her way down the staircase that led to the cells.

Hunter was still separated from the pack, and Lilly assumed he would be the least cooperative anyway. She ignored his cell and opened the one where Gavin, Matthew, Teri, and Chloe resided.

"I'm gonna make this simple," Lilly said in a calm, cool tone. "Here is a list of places that Koyt has been known to hole up in. The first one to give me information that turns into a real lead lives. The others will end up like him."

She dumped her parcel open and body parts began to roll toward the criminals. Chloe and Terri shrieked as Red's head tumbled toward their feet.

Lilly regretted the action as soon as she had done it, but it was too late to turn back now. "You have five minutes," she added before turning toward the door.

Lilly stumbled backwards a step as she stared into Tread's horrified eyes.

He pushed past her and rapidly collected the remains of his friend, glaring at Lilly as he exited.

Lilly turned back to the cell once more. "The clock is ticking."

When she had decided to use Red's body as a scare tactic, Lilly couldn't tell him. It all just happened. She definitely hadn't meant for Tread to see it.

She rushed after him and stopped short upstairs as he carefully wrapped the remains back in the worn tablecloths.

"Tread—"

"Just don't," he spat back angrily. "There are no words for what you just did."

"I brought him back for you," she added hastily.

"For me," he balked. "Oh, I can see that."

"I'm sorry. I didn't plan that. I found him and thought you'd like to give him a proper burial. But Red is dead. And if the situation were reversed and my dead corpse could help save the someone's life, I would want to do it. And I think Red would too." All of her excuses and rationalizations sounded weaker as she spoke them versus when she had thought of them.

"You knew him for like five minutes. How do you know what he would have wanted? Even if it was okay, you should have given me a warning." He kept his back to her. "Since you're done, I'm going to go bury my friend now. Don't follow me," he added.

Lilly watched as he strode out of the prison.

A whistle came from her right.

"Wow, that was cold." Mark shook his head. "Even I wouldn't have let you desecrate that kid."

Lilly sighed, cupping her face in her hands. "I know!" she exclaimed in frustration. She collapsed into an empty chair. "My mind is just in a state of fog. I wasn't thinking clearly. I regretted it as soon as I had done it." She looked up at Mark for any sign of understanding but was greeted with none. "I just want my mom back. And my mind keeps going to the deepest, darkest places. I have no clue what Koyt could be doing to her as we speak. But you're right, I crossed a line and if I continue to disregard my friends' counsel and barrel ahead guns blazing, I may not recognize myself if...no," she shook her head, "not if, *when* I find my mom. I can't let myself go there."

Lilly jumped to her feet. "I need to talk to Tread," she said more to herself than to Mark as she darted out of the prison.

"You might want to give him time to cool off!" Mark called after her.

He was probably offering her sound advice. But the lump in her stomach was growing. She had gone too far, and Tread needed to hear that. He might still be upset and need time to process her apology, but at least he would have heard it. That's what she should have begun with in the first place instead of foolishly trying to get him to believe something even she didn't believe.

Lilly spotted him over in the southeast fields, standing under a towering oak tree that was at least a hundred years old. Annie stood beside him. They each carried a shovel.

"Just make her leave. I can't do this right now," Tread said quietly to Annie as they heard Lilly approach.

Annie stepped forward to meet her.

"Now's not the right time."

"I know," Lilly admitted. "I'm sorry. My mind isn't right. I keep imagining the horrible things Koyt is doing to my mother and nothing else has mattered. I went too far."

Tread stood stiff with his back towards her. His body language gave no indication that he was listening, but she knew he could hear her.

"I'm filled with all this rage. I don't know what to do with it. I just know," Lilly looked toward Tread, willing him to turn around, "I don't want to become a monster like Koyt. I want to get through this and still have the people I love—the people that love me—recognize me when this is over."

Lilly looked back at Annie. "Pay my respects to Red. I hope he can forgive me. He was one of a kind and didn't deserve this. We were on our way to becoming fast friends." Then Lilly added quietly, "I'm sorry, Red," before turning to leave.

"Wait," Tread called.

She stopped and turned back.

"Look, I'm still mad, but I've been where you've been. The darkness can just overtake you to where nothing else matters."

She was pretty sure he was referring to the time in his life when his sister had been murdered by Lilly's father.

"When it's over, even if you can make it back to the person you were, or a better version of that…," He half smiled, and Lilly knew he was giving her the credit for the changes he'd made, "it still haunts you." He stepped closer and took her hand in his. "Lilly, I love you. If you can trust nothing else, trust that. I don't want you to have things in your past that will plague you for the rest of your existence."

"I know. I'm sorry." She wrapped her arms around him and kissed him on the cheek. "I need you to be my touchstone like you've always been." She leaned back, looking in his eyes. "I promise I will listen from now on."

Lilly stood back silently as Annie and Tread dug a deep grave for Red, feeling like an intruder and wondering if Red would even want her present.

It was heartbreaking to watch Tread carefully arrange his friend back together, his body still perfectly preserved. Red's eyes still held the betrayal and shock he must have felt when Koyt ended his existence. Annie covered his body in a red piece of silk fabric before she and Tread took turns pouring shovels full of earth into the grave.

Once the grave was filled, Annie laid a small bundle of white roses on top.

"We'll have to make a headstone later," Tread noted as he kneeled down beside the grave. "I'm so sorry, Red. Your death is on me. I know me admitting it does nothing for you. I should have seen the evil in Koyt. I should have listened to those around me." He gave an apologetic look to Lilly. "You brought so much happiness into my life.

You were like a son to me, and I failed you." He clenched his hand into a fist and pounded the dirt beside the grave. "I can't change the past. If I could trade places with you I would. All I can do is promise you that *he* will pay for this. I will forever miss you, my friend."

He stood up and brushed the dirt off of his pants and reached for Lilly's hand.

She shook her head. "Can I have a minute?" she asked, uncertain if she deserved it.

He nodded. "I'll meet you back at my place."

After Annie and Tread were out of sight, Lilly turned back to the freshly dug grave.

"I don't know if you even want me here, but I wanted to say thank you. Red, I knew you for such a little amount of time, but kindness radiated from you. You saved, Ryan, my parents, heck you probably saved half of the town. Thank you for going to get the medicine even though I know you knew what kind of psycho Koyt was. I know you tried to warn me. And when you didn't come back, I knew for certain that Koyt was the sociopath I had believed him to be. You didn't deserve this. I'm sorry for my fault in all this. I hope you are up there living in some kind of paradise." She kissed her fingers and then touched the top of the dirt where she thought his head would be.

Tread was actually not in his apartment when she arrived but waiting for her on the front steps of the building. Lilly still felt ashamed for her actions with Red's remains and felt awkward near Tread.

But when he slipped his hand into hers, it all faded away. "Come on," he said, tugging her forward.

"Where are we going?"

"To the jail. We need to see if that stunt of yours worked."

She pulled her hand back. "Tread, come on. I said I was sorry. I don't want to be that person."

He gently cupped her face in his hands. "I know, and you're not. You made a mistake. You're not a monster, Lilly. But it's already been done and Red wouldn't want us to let that go to waste. Maybe it rattled one of them enough to yield us some valuable intel." Then he raised his eyebrow in his cocky signature move, and Lilly knew she had truly been forgiven. "Now, are you coming or do I have to sling you over my shoulder like Tarzan and take you with me?"

She rolled her eyes. "Let's go."

The jail was quiet when they arrived.

Mark was sitting at the desk and greeted them with a death stare when they arrived. Lilly had never seen him so angry.

Tread laughed. "Um, was it my shift next and I forgot to come switch with you?"

He pushed his chair back from the table, clearly annoyed, stood, and leaned forward. "Next time you want to try some harebrained scheme," he pointed his finger at Lilly, "you'd better be the one to stick around for the aftermath," he growled.

"What happened?" Lilly asked, trying to suppress a laugh at the look of rage on Mark's face.

"It was like a circus down there. Screaming and fighting about who got to talk first. They bloody nearly killed each other. I had to separate them by couples or Gavin and Matthew would have killed each other." He shook his head. "And yeah, after that, I think it *is* your turn to take over. Takin' on four vamps at once." He shook his head angrily. "The only thing that kept them from escaping or taking me on was the thought that I still had a sunwalker or two upstairs."

It was hard not to laugh. Lilly had never seen Mark so upset—his whole body was quivering. He was typically just indifferent or bored. But as he stormed past them, roughly shoving in between them as he went, Lilly actually bit down on her tongue to keep a laugh from escaping.

Tread on the other hand didn't even try and suppress his smile. When she glanced at him, he had a big goofy grin splayed across his face.

She nudged him in the ribcage with her elbow.

"Come on, we shouldn't laugh," she began to say, but before she could finish a giggle escaped her lips.

He raised an eyebrow at her hypocrisy.

Then she straightened her face. "I didn't say I didn't think it was funny. I've never seen so much emotion from Mark. I just said we shouldn't laugh. Taking on four vampires isn't fair. We really need to expand the prison, and if we're going to have more than one person to a cell then we need to add more guards."

"That's a nice idea in theory, but after the whole coup, we are a little thin when it comes to vampires. And I don't think we want to pull someone from a wall."

She hit him somewhat hard.

"Hey, what was that for?" he exclaimed, more out of curiosity than anything else.

"It's a little aggravating to have you be right so often."

"So often?" he asked, pretending to have wounded feelings. "When am I wrong?"

She rolled her eyes.

"Come on, Mr. Right." Lilly said sarcastically, pulling his shirt forward. "Let's see what these traitors were so eager to share that they were fighting each other to be the one who got to tell us."

A vibration in her pocket startled Lilly. She reached in and pulled out the phone Ryan had sent her after Koyt had mysteriously lost the first one.

"It's Ryan." She gestured down the stairs. "You go ahead and find out if any of them really know anything. I need to take this. Maybe he found out how to help Lex."

She touched the screen to answer and held the phone gently to her ear.

"Ryan."

"Lilly, how are things going? Any word on your mom?"

"No, not yet. We are still looking for any clue as to where Koyt could have taken her. How is your search coming? Did you find a place to get Lex treatment?"

There was a long pause. Lilly wondered if the connection had been dropped somehow.

"Ryan?" she asked again.

"I'm still here…Lilly, I'm sorry. I've struck out. It's hard to pull in favors when people are terrified to trust me. The last group who did ended up dead and my missing arm is a constant reminder of that fact to anyone I approach. I could clear out a building and get equipment but there would be no one to treat her."

"We can't give up," Lilly insisted. "Maybe Adam can read up on treatments and do it himself?"

"Lilly, I don't think it works like that. From what I know, treatments are usually modified for each individual case. Adam just doesn't have the expertise. I'll keep looking but don't get your hopes up. Unless you know another doctor…"

"I do!" Lilly said as an idea suddenly popped into her head.

"Is he an oncologist?"

"No, at least I don't think so, but maybe he knows someone. He's brilliant, has several degrees…but I need you to get me his number. This particular doctor works for the government."

"Okay," Ryan said hesitantly. "I can probably find a number. What's the doctor's name?"

"Dr. Eric Crews."

"Crews…that name sounds familiar."

"It's Lex's father. He's some scientist for the government. I don't know exactly what he does, but I know he'd do anything for his daughter. Maybe someone will trust him enough to help."

"Give me a few hours and I'll send you a number."

"Thanks, Ryan. I know you don't have to help us, so thank you."

"Let me know if you get any leads on Koyt."

"I will. He won't get away with this."

Lilly hung up the phone just as Tread was reemerging from the downstairs cells.

"Anything useful?"

Tread shrugged. "That remains to be seen. Vanessa's list was long and extensive. Koyt traveled a ton over the years. There are fifteen locations that they claim to have heard Koyt mention." He handed her the paper. "Of course Hunter is still being tight-lipped. I would have a bit more confidence if he named a place. Koyt was closer to him than the others."

Lilly nodded in acknowledgement as she scanned the paper. Out of the hundreds of places on the list the cities that were highlighted were

KOWLOON

VENICE

DENVER

ALBANY

MEXICO CITY

BEIJING

TAMPA

TUCUMCARI

OKLAHOMA CITY

SAN ANTONIO

SÃO PAULO

MONTERREY

PHOENIX

OKLAHOMA CITY

PARIS

CARSON CITY

"Well, I recognize most of these…but Kowloon? Where is that?"
"Hong Kong, if I'm not mistaken," Tread guessed.
"At least it's a start."
Tread shrugged. "Or they just randomly circled names."
Lilly sighed in frustration. "Well the list did come from Vanessa. So we know he has stayed in these locations before. It's something to go on, so I'm going to hope they are being truthful. Because a list of fifteen cities is far more manageable than this." She waved the sheet of paper that had column after column of cities.

"It's something," Tread agreed, reaching for the paper. "I'll take it over to Vanessa and see if she remembers any more details about these exact locations, like maybe an address."

"Wouldn't that be lovely. Meet me back at your place. I'm famished, and I just can't face my dad right now. Not until I know something more." Lilly rubbed her eyes.

"That's perfectly fine by me." He leaned forward and kissed her on the forehead. "You should probably go and get a few hours of sleep as well."

"No." She shook her head adamantly. "No, after Vanessa gives us what she knows, I'm starting on the list."

"You won't do any good for your mother if you collapse from

exhaustion. Besides, we should wait until Ryan calls you back and then it will take a little time to get supplies together."

Fifteen cities, even if the right one was buried in the list, could take months to comb through. Most of the cities were majorly populated and spread out across the globe. Any delay could mean the death of her mother, if her mother was even still alive.

Vanessa had assured her that Koyt liked to take his time with his victims in order to extract every ounce of revenge possible. But sending her on a wild goose chase, searching the globe for someone whom he had already killed, seemed equally sadistic and right up Koyt's alley to Lilly.

She pushed the thought away. Her mind couldn't go there. Hope was all that was holding her together right now. She couldn't afford to lose it.

"All right," she finally relented through a yawn. "Wake me in three hours."

Tread looked like he might argue but then nodded. He kissed her quickly on the lips and then disappeared outside.

There was a noticeable change in the atmosphere of Spero as she walked outside. It was eerily quiet. Based on the position of the sun in the sky, it had to be close to noon. Normally people would be outside, talking, laughing, on their way to their shifts or coming home for lunch breaks.

The few people Lilly did pass on the street were nervous, looking over their shoulders and hurrying to their destinations. It was as if they were all afraid that Koyt could be hiding around the next turn.

And why shouldn't they be afraid? It's not as if she or Tread could protect them from the world's most ancient vampire. The only way they even had a chance of protecting themselves was with Steel's sword. Koyt had bested them both and would have ended their existences had it not been for Vanessa arriving in the nick of time.

Koyt had shocked them all by attacking Tread at dusk and revealing to Spero that he was a sunwalker. He easily beaten Tread as they fought one on one. Koyt's goons had kept Lilly from interfering. Koyt almost beheaded Tread, crushing his way through Tread's windpipe with his shoe. If Vanessa hadn't arrived at the last second wielding Steel's sword, Tread would be dead now. Lilly shuddered at the memory. She never wanted to be that close to losing the love of her life ever again.

As she slowly climbed the stairs to Tread's apartment a horrific thought entered her mind.

What if Koyt's entire plan was to wait for her and Tread to leave? He could easily slaughter the whole community. They would be defenseless without the blade and without a sunwalker. But if Lilly and Tread didn't take the dragon steel sword with them, they wouldn't stand a chance to kill a vampire who had been alive for almost a millennium. Even with the sword, their chance of survival was minimum.

The apartment was quiet when Lilly reached the door. She opened it, relieved to not have to face her uncle and more questions she didn't have answers to.

After downing a blood bag, she crawled into Tread's bed and wrapped herself in the comforter. She could feel the exhaustion fighting to overtake her, but the anxiety of everything happening kept her mind from letting it win.

She tried to push everything aside, but thoughts of doom kept pushing their way through. Finally, Lilly decided to try to focus on a memory, a good one. She thought back to the first time she and Lex met and as she remembered the happiness she felt at finally having a real friend, the exhaustion finally won and sleep overtook her.

The sound of hushed voices jarred Lilly from her slumber. As she stretched and regained her senses, she could feel the energy flowing through her. She felt completely revitalized and knew that Tread had not kept his word. This was not the result of a three-hour nap.

"Whether you whisper or not, I can still hear you," Lilly said as she walked out to find a group of vampires and one lone human huddled around the kitchen table. Sam, Scott, Annie, Tread, and her uncle were all looking down at a map of the United States.

"Well, I am nothing if not a gentleman." Tread smiled.

"Gentlemen keep their word and wake people after three hours," Lilly countered back sarcastically.

Tread looked appalled. "That was an honest mistake. I got caught up in discussion with our friends here and the time must have just slipped past me unnoticed. I offer you my most sincere heartfelt apologies," he lied unconvincingly.

"How could I have ever doubted you?" Lilly rolled her eyes as she made her way to the table.

Tread and Sam scooted to the side to make room for her.

"That's what I keep asking myself." He smirked.

"So, what did I miss?" Lilly asked with a big yawn as she looked down at the map that had tiny multicolored pins sticking out of it.

"We were just discussing the best route for you guys to travel on your search," Adam said as he pointed south on the map. "We think you should start here, in San Antonio. It's close and then it's just a short trip down to Monterrey or over to Tucumcari and then Phoenix."

"I've been thinking about this. I am going to be making this trip solo. Tread will stay here."

"Absolutely not!" Tread exclaimed at the same time that Uncle Adam said, "No way, Lil."

"Listen, I know what you're going to say, but you both haven't thought this through."

"There is nothing you can say. NOTHING," Tread enunciated the word slowly, "that would convince me to allow you to do this on your own." He rubbed his recently healed neck. "You saw what he did to me, and I am much older than you Lil."

"What if *he's* just waiting for us to leave?" Lilly began raising her voice heatedly. "Isn't that just what a sick, evil maniac like Koyt would do? Come in and slaughter everyone while we're gone looking for my mom? Only then to just kill her, too. That's what Vanessa said he does, takes everything away from you that matters."

"Lil—"

"No! I am not going to underestimate him again. Look at where that has gotten us." She looked to Sam and Scott. "What do you think? How safe will you feel here guarding the town with both sunwalkers gone and a lunatic on a rampage?"

Sam looked down uncomfortably.

Scott stayed silent for a brief second, then looked up apologetically at Tread.

"I'm sorry, Tread. But Lilly's right. We all have people we love here." He interlaced his fingers with Sam's and squeezed them affectionately. "I think Lilly's fears are reasonable and need to be addressed. If she's right, you both will be away and safe and we will be the ones to pay for any ill-made decisions."

"Okay. You're right," Tread acknowledged. "I guess we do need to think this through a little better. But," he looked seriously at Lilly, "I

know the answer isn't to send you off on your own."

The room fell silent as each of them considered new alternatives.

"What about Vanessa?" Annie suggested. "Will she stay here the entire time you both are gone?"

The tension seemed to roll off Tread as he heard his friend's idea. "I'm sure she would if I asked her."

"And are you planning on leaving the dragon steel sword here?" Scott asked. "Because they may be siblings," he paused for verification, and waited until Tread nodded before he continued, "but he is still a sunwalker. None of us stand a chance against him without a weapon." He rubbed his chin. "No scenario is going to be perfect. There is still a huge risk to us, even if Vanessa stays and is armed to the nines. If he strikes in daylight, she is severely limited in her response."

"But if they leave us the weapon and Koyt doesn't come here, how do you both have any chance of defeating him without the dragon steel?" Sam asked, her voice laced with concern.

"We'll just have to find another weapon," Lilly answered.

"I thought these weapons were incredibly rare?" Adam asked, leaning forward.

Tread sighed. "They are. But I don't think we have any other options. And I know where we can arm ourselves."

This last statement brought everyone's heads up.

"Where?" Annie asked.

"Looks like we'll just have to raid a VAS storage site." Tread smiled weakly.

"That's suicide," Scott interjected.

"You can't be serious," Sam added.

"Your mother won't want you to die for her, Lilly. No parent would," Adam explained.

"There has to be another option," Annie insisted.

Lilly nodded to Tread.

"We'll make it work. Maybe Ryan can help," she hoped out loud.

After an awkward silence, Lilly was filled in on the rest of the proposed plan. The international spots had been crossed off the list. With time ticking away, they had decided the best option would be to check as many of the destinations as possible, but anything oversees would be harder for Koyt to travel to with Elaine in tow. Typically, vampires would just swim across the ocean, but traveling with a human along would be problematic. If Koyt wanted to bring Lilly's mother to one of the further locations he would have to go through more conventional options. Flights were rare, especially international ones. The security was on high alert, so the probability that Koyt would choose that route was minimal.

Mexico was the only out-of-the-country spot that they were considering, since it could be reached on foot.

After the meeting, Scott approached Lilly.

"I'm sorry about Steel's weapon. Wanting it to stay here makes things a lot more dangerous for you."

She shook her head. "Scott, there is nothing to apologize for. I want everyone to be safe. I've been having the same concerns. I love my mom, but there are still plenty of people here I care about. You and Sam are included in that." She gave him a hug. "Really, I should be thanking you."

He took a step back, looking confused.

"This whole mess was caused because of choices Tread and I made. It is our fault Spero is in danger. It would be easy and maybe the sane thing to do," she chuckled, "to just cut bait and run. But you and Sam, Annie, Mark…everyone. You are all staying and risking everything to protect this town."

Sam walked up beside her mate. "That's because we believe in this place. And in you. Lilly, you have showed us that things we never even would have dreamed of are possible. These last few months, we've been at peace, living without constantly looking over our shoulder. It has been paradise."

Scott wrapped his arm around her. "We'll do our best to keep things in order while you're gone. I just wish we could send you out there better protected."

Chapter IV

A GIFT

After the meeting had adjourned, Tread dragged Lilly to find Henry. The engineer had apparently been working on something for them to take on the journey. Tread was being very tight-lipped about the whole project.

They were just about to enter Town Hall, where Henry's office, or more appropriate, his workshop, was located, when Lilly's phone dinged.

There was a single text.

728-3539

"Was he able to locate the number?" Tread asked.

"Looks like it. Wish me luck?"

"Always."

Punching in seven digits never seemed so daunting. Lilly didn't know what her next step would be if Lex's father couldn't pull off a miracle. Other options were nonexistent.

The number rang and rang and rang. Finally on the fourth ring he answered. "This is Dr. Crews."

"Dr. Crews, please don't hang up. I need you to listen. Your daughter's life is at stake and I can't risk this call being traced."

"Lilly." His voice was filled with disdain. "Why should I be shocked that a vampire would threaten my daughter. I did wonder about you though. I thought maybe there was a chance you were different. After all, you had years filled with opportunities if you wanted to harm her, or us for that matter. But I guess it's just part of your nature. What do you want?"

Although Dr. Crews was rarely at home throughout Lex's childhood, it still stung to hear even him doubt Lilly's intentions. She had countless sleepovers with his daughter and had ample occasions to hurt any of them throughout the years. Why would she suddenly turn into a monster?

Dr. Crews's rant had already taken up far too much of their precious time. So Lilly had no time to sugarcoat the situation or ease into it.

"Lex has leukemia," she blurted out. "She's on the VAS's most wanted list and I need you to find a way to get her treatment. I'm out of time. I will call you again tomorrow."

"No wait—" he yelled as Lilly hung up the phone.

"That was quick," Tread noted. "I mean, you didn't give him much time to give you any answers, let alone ask any questions."

"I know." Lilly pulled open the door to the building. "Henry said to keep calls short or they could be traced. I can't take any chances."

Tread stepped in after her and they made their way to the engineer's workroom.

He was busy tinkering away at a table filled with wires and parts. Lilly wondered how on earth all that could ever turn into anything useful, but her mind didn't work the same way as Henry's.

The workshop smelled of burnt metal and stale air.

We really need to get him a fan, or a room with windows," Lilly thought as she scrunched up her nose, wondering how the engineer could stand it.

"I was wondering when you were going to get here," Henry said as he put down a small soldering iron. "You told me to put a rush on these, and I was beginning to think you had changed your mind." He brushed his hands off on his pants and stepped out from behind the table he was working on.

"So, were you successful?" Tread asked excitedly.

A look of annoyance flashed on the engineer's face as he reached to his left under a small table and pulled out two backpacks.

"It was never a question of my capabilities. I just wasn't absolutely sure about the timetable," he clarified. "But yes, I finished them with time to spare. I even just finished my first prototype of our very own satellite phone." He beamed proudly. "But we can talk about that later."

He handed one backpack to each of them. Lilly took the blue one, leaving the gray one for Tread. The material wasn't as pliable as a typical bag. It was lined with a sort of stiff plastic.

"Those should both insulate a half-dozen blood bags. Just be careful with them. I have done my best to stabilize all the parts," he smiled a satisfactory grin, but then grew serious, "but it can still break."

"So it's like a mini refrigerator?" Lilly asked in awe.

"It's a little more complicated than that, but yes, I guess you could call it that. Just don't go dropping it or jumping off buildings with it. Too much friction could cause it to malfunction."

Lilly unzipped it and looked inside. There was a little hatch at the top of the bag and when she lifted it, cold air came pouring out.

"Incredible!" Lilly leaned forward and kissed Henry on the cheek. "You are brilliant. This is going to really help us as we search for my mom. We won't have to double back as often."

"When do you leave?" Henry asked.

"We still have a few things we need to work out, but hopefully in a day or two." Tread slid the backpack over his right shoulder and glanced over to a far table in the back that had a small black object on it. "So, is that the phone you mentioned?"

"Yes," Henry said as he turned to see what his friend was looking at. He picked it up and handed it to Tread.

"And it works?"

"It should. I just need to call a number to test it out."

"Try calling Lilly's phone," he suggested.

"You have a phone?" Henry asked in a somewhat accusatory tone. Tread turned to Lilly, "You never told him?"

"I just never got around to it," she answered sheepishly. "We have had a lot going on here," she added in her defense.

"Do you know how much work you could have saved me, if I had a functioning phone to work off of." He waved the phone in front of her in frustration. Then he sighed. "Oh well, never mind now. Let's test it."

Henry dialed Lilly's phone number and to her and Tread's astonishment it rang.

"Now we will be able to check in and keep you updated on our search." Lilly felt the relief wash over her. She wouldn't have to wonder if everyone here was safe too.

"So, Lilly told me we need to keep the calls brief. How short are we talking?"

Before answering, Henry walked back behind his large work table and pulled out a weird looking device.

"It's not finished yet. And now I will need to make two," he held up a finger, "but if it works, this should be able to clip onto the back of the phone like this." He demonstrated his new gadget by sliding it onto the back of his phone. "This will then activate when you make a call. It should scramble the signal and give you at least five minutes, maybe more." He shrugged. "I just need to finish working on an algorithm that will keep the signal bouncing."

"Just how smart are you?" Lilly asked in jest.

"Well, where do you think Einstein got his theory of relativity from?" Henry retorted back seriously.

Lilly's jaw dropped open. "No way!"

Henry laughed. "I'm not quite that old." He stuck his hand out. "I'll need your phone too."

Lilly held on to it reluctantly.

"If you want me to make a scrambler for it, I need both so I can try them out, see how long I can keep the trace searching for our location before it locks on. With one phone it's a lot of hypothesizing and hoping for the best. With two, my accuracy will increase one hundred-fold."

He tapped his foot impatiently.

"Lilly, I am going to give the phone back."

"It's not that," she insisted. "I'm just working on something and I need to stay in contact with certain people. Lex is sick and I'm trying to get her the treatment she needs."

"If you need to use it, it will be here. I'm not going to take it apart or break it."

Handing over the phone was harder than Lilly thought it would be. She knew Henry was brilliant and chances were everything would be fine. But it was her only link to the outside world. The phone was her one chance at helping save Lex's life.

"Okay," she said, carefully handing him the phone. "Just be careful."

"Even if something happened to it—" he began, and Lilly's eyess widened in horror. "It's won't!" Henry added quickly. "I'm just saying *if* it did. Now we know that I can make another one."

Lilly let the tension release from her body that she hadn't realized she had been holding in.

"You're right. Thanks, Henry."

"I'm going to run to the clinic and talk to Annie. See how much blood we can take in these. You should probably go visit your father. Update him. I'm sure he's going crazy and I am the last person he wants to see right now." Tread leaned forward and gave her a quick kiss before disappearing.

She had been hoping that she wouldn't have to see her dad until Elaine was found. An unrealistic dream, but one she had been wishing for nonetheless.

"Okay, I guess I will see you later, Henry."

"Wait," Henry called. "I wanted to ask you something."

Curiosity piqued, Lilly waited.

"Are you really going after Koyt without Lord Steel's sword?"

By the look on his face, Lilly could tell he thought she and Tread were crazy.

"We need to leave the city protected. We're going to attempt to break into a VAS warehouse."

"I want you to take this with you." Henry stepped behind a table and slid open a drawer, pulling out something wrapped in a red cloth.

He unwrapped it carefully. "I found this…well, let's just say a long time ago. I don't advertise it." He pushed a small, curved dagger into her hand. The hilt was gold and ornately decorated.

"Are those rubies?" Lilly asked.

"I believe so. I never got it appraised," he teased.

"This is edged with dragon steel, just like the sword," she noted after a more careful examination.

"Yes."

"And you're giving it to me?" Lilly asked, knowing the worth of the item she was holding.

"Loaning it," he corrected. "It's smaller, so you will have to get a lot closer to Koyt, putting you in more danger than the sword would put you in. But I can't have you out there unprotected. I know you say the council runs the city. And perhaps they do. But we all know it would fall apart without you."

"I don't know what to say. I mean, thank you, obviously. This will make me feel a lot safer."

"Don't thank me, just make sure you bring it back." He squeezed her hand gently.

She could tell what he really meant was for her to come back.

She gave him a hug. "What would we do without you, Henry?"

"Let's not find out." He chuckled to himself.

When Lilly arrived in the hallway that led to her apartment, she stopped. To the right was Tread and Uncle Adam's place and to the left was her father. She knew eventually a conversation would have to take place. But procrastination seemed so much more appealing at the moment. Pushing the guilt aside she strode into her uncle's apartment.

It was empty, the map still spread across the table. Although the dagger that was tucked away carefully in her boot did offer her some comfort, it was not enough.

She had underestimated Koyt enough. They would still need to raid a VAS facility. Koyt was cunning. He was stronger, faster, and had more fighting experience than they did. Plus, he was ruthless. The only way they would win this fight was if they were better equipped. And if Henry had a dragon steel weapon, what was to stop Koyt from having accumulated one or two in his long lifetime?

Breaking into a VAS facility would not be a simple task. Reinforcement would be needed. Alex was their closest and only ally. She had returned to Little Rock, her home, the night before. Hopefully she and her friends would be willing to help them. Little Rock had two VAS warehouses. One of those would be the target. Hopefully one was less secure than the other.

The calendar on her uncle's wall caught her attention. Alex had said they had twenty-five days until the next full moon. Now they were down to twenty-three. Just over three weeks. And after crossing off any locations that required them to cross an ocean, they still had eleven cities to explore, not to mention travel time.

Time was slipping through her fingers. It didn't matter what preparations were unfinished. She was leaving in the morning whether Tread was ready or not.

She had put off her father long enough. He deserved to be updated, and besides, there were things in her apartment she needed to pack.

Dylan was sitting on the couch when Lilly entered. His head was bandaged and he was staring at the wall. He didn't appear to have heard her come in.

"Dad?" Lilly called softly, not wanting to startle him.

He turned around and met her with blank, bloodshot eyes. It looked like her father hadn't slept since Elaine's abduction, but there seemed to be no recollection there.

"Dad?" she called a second time, as she stepped around the couch, moving closer to him.

It took a moment but he finally seemed to snap out of whatever trance he was in.

"Did you find her?" he asked, looking around wildly. "Where's Elaine?"

This was worse than she had imagined. She had expected the overwhelming guilt for failing her mother to intensify when she saw her father, and it did. But she hadn't expected to find him in this condition.

"Not yet. But I am leaving tomorrow with—" she started to say, but quickly thought better of mentioning Tread, "I'm leaving tomorrow. I have a list of locations to search. I will find mom. I promise you."

Mentioning Tread's name was probably not the best thing at the moment. Her father was already on edge.

She reached forward to pat her father on the shoulder, to try to comfort him but he pulled back.

Dylan blamed her too. Lilly knew she deserved it—it was her fault—but it still hurt to see her father pull away from her.

Lilly tried to conceal the hurt in her eyes. She went to the kitchen and made her father a turkey sandwich. It didn't look like he had eaten anything since Adam had brought him back from the hospital.

"You need to eat something," she insisted as she set the plate on the coffee table in from of him. "If not for me, do it for mom. What will she do if you have withered away to nothing by the time she comes home?"

Without acknowledging his daughter, he picked up the sandwich and took a small bite before returning it to the plate.

Leaving her father to his thoughts, Lilly went into her room to pack.

Traveling light was a necessity. Every second counted and Lilly didn't want anything to slow her down.

There was enough space in her mini-fridge backpack for a change of clothes and some personal hygiene items.

She changed into beige jeans and a t-shirt and grabbed a zip-up hoodie. The weather was just starting to cool down. The hoodie would help her look inconspicuous in the cities, as well as help conceal her face. It was plastered on the news daily from what Alex had told her.

A quick knock on the door pulled Lilly out of her thoughts. She glanced at her dad's plate as she went to open the door. A second bite had been taken, but judging by how far away the plate had been pushed, it looked like he wasn't planning on eating any more.

Lilly was surprised to see Henry when she opened the door, having only left him an hour or two ago.

"Just wanted to return this." He smiled reassuringly as he pushed the phone towards her.

"Don't you need it to make the signal scrambler thing?"

"I finished that. It was quite simple once I had two phones to test it on. Replicating it took no time at all once I had all the mechanics worked out." He shrugged as if it were as easy as flipping on a light switch. "Anyway, I knew how anxious you were without it."

"Thanks." Lilly smiled, happy to be a step closer to leaving in the morning. She flipped the phone over and noticed he had slid a small black device on the back of the phone. "So, this is it?" she asked. "How long can I talk for? Five minutes?"

"After testing it against my algorithm, I would say you are safe for at least ten minutes, and that is *if* they tried to trace it. Maybe they won't. But for safety's sake, let's just say ten minutes."

Lilly nodded. Ten minutes was more than she ever dreamt possible. She might actually be able to have a conversation with Dr. Crews.

"Thanks," she repeated.

Henry gave her a curt nod before disappearing down the hallway. Lilly stepped in the corridor and shut the door behind her. Ten minutes. She had said that she would call Lex's dad tomorrow, but now that she had more time she didn't want to wait. If there was something he could do to help, she needed to know now. Before she and Tread left town.

Lilly called the last number dialed from the phone. It was answered before it could ring twice.

"Don't hang up, Lilly." The doctor's voice sounded desperate.

"I have more time now. Don't bother with a trace. I have ten minutes and not a second more."

"I won't. Just tell me the truth. Does Lex really have leukemia? How would you even know?"

Lilly related the story of the epidemic that spread through the town, how they all thought Lex was relapsing, and how they obtained the results.

"You need to get Lex to me. I can help her."

"You're an oncologist? I thought you were some sort of Dr. Frankenstein working on secret experiments for the government."

He sighed. "I do that. But I have several degrees, and countless connections."

"You won't be able to just walk her into a hospital. She is on the VAS most-wanted list."

"The government will give me anything I ask for, equipment-wise. I have facilities in several different states. That's why I travel so much. I have an old colleague who I worked with before I started with the government. She's one the best oncologists around." He paused. "I would do anything for my daughter. I want to believe you would too."

"Of course I would."

"Just get her to me. I will handle the rest. You owe her that much. She's in this mess because she was friends with you."

"I know," Lilly agreed.

There was a moment of silence before he asked, "Did she know? I mean before all this, did she know you were a vampire?"

"Yes. She's known…always."

"Okay. Tell me where you are and I will see how close I can get."

"No, I can't tell you that."

"I'm not going to tell anyone. I just want my daughter!" he cried, raising his voice.

"I can tell you where she will be."

"Fine. Where can you bring her?" he asked hotly.

"I can't bring her. I have other obligations. But I will send her there with someone I trust."

"No. For all I know Lex is dead and this is a trap. If you want me to come, if this story is really true and Lex is your best friend…well, then you would be the one to bring her."

It would cost her at least another day. Either way a life was at stake, Lex or her mother. If Koyt truly wanted to torture Lilly and turn Elaine into a darkwalker then she still had three weeks. From what Adam had told her, every day Lex didn't get treatment was like a ticking time bomb. He didn't have the resources to see how aggressive the cancer was.

"Fine. You're right. I will bring her. But if this is a trap, it won't end well for you."

"Come alone, just you and Lex, or I'll leave. I don't know what to believe but I'm not willing to risk my daughter's life over it."

"Deal. Tomorrow at noon. I'll text you an address in Arkansas. Can you get there that soon?"

"I'll be there," Dr. Crews promised before hanging up.

Arkansas was her destination anyway. Taking Lex would cost them some time but not a lot. Plus, meeting in another state would help keep Spero safe in case Dr. Crews's intentions weren't one hundred percent pure.

Now all she needed to do was convince Ethan to let Lex go and tell Tread their timeline was now locked in place. Hopefully he had accomplished everything he needed to do today.

Chapter V

LEAVING

She was greeted at the door with a pounce and a big hug.

"Lilly!" Luke squealed.

"Hey buddy, how are you doing?" she asked while ruffling his hair with one hand and tickling him with the other.

He laughed and laughed, unable to answer her question.

When Lex popped her head out of the bedroom, Lilly let Luke breathe.

"Hey." Her friend waved before bending down to pick up multi-colored blocks that were scattered across the floor.

"What happened here?" Lilly bent down to help her.

"A tornado!" Ethan exclaimed triumphantly.

"It must have been a big one," Lilly noted from how far the blocks were spread out over the room.

The bedroom door opened wider and Ethan stepped out.

"Hey Lilly." he nodded before turning his attention to Luke. "Are you ready to head out?"

"Let's go feed piggies!" Luke jumped up and down excitedly.

"Actually, can I talk to you both before you leave?" she asked, glancing at Luke.

Taking the hint, Ethan nudged Luke into the bedroom. "Before we go you need to make your bed and pick up your area."

"Okay," Luke agreed sullenly.

After shutting the door and helping Lex off of the floor, Ethan turned back to Lilly.

"What has happened now?"

"If you haven't told him yet, you need to now," Lilly insisted.

Lex's eyes went wide with horror, as Ethan turned to his wife.

"Told me what?" he asked.

"Lilly, this is not your business," she began as tears filled her eyes.

"Lex, I wish I had more time to give you, but I think I found you a way to get treated and we have to leave in the morning."

Ethan whipped his head back and forth between the two women.

"Will someone tell me what's going on?" he demanded.

Lex tried to explain between sobs but was mostly incoherent.

"Lex has leukemia," Lilly finally explained. "She wanted to wait to tell you when there was hope and now there is."

"Cancer?" Ethan asked in disbelief, as he wrapped his arms around his wife and held her tight. "You said it was just some residual effects from Hib."

"I'm sorry," she cried, leaning into him more.

"So, you got her treatment. Okay," Ethan said, trying to stay strong. "I'll get us packed. Where are we going?"

"Not you, just Lex."

"If you think I'm sending my wife off with strangers to treat this, you're crazy. I know she's on the VAS list. Outside these walls, she's a target. I am going with her."

Lilly softened her voice. "Ethan, if there were another way then I would be happy to let you come. The terms are simple. If we want help, it's just Lex. As you said, she's on the VAS list. Finding someone and the equipment to help her isn't easy. I don't have other options. It's this or nothing."

"No!" Ethan yelled, hanging onto his wife desperately.

"Lex will be in good hands. The doctor won't let anything happen to her."

"How can you promise that?" Ethan asked in astonishment.

"Because it's her father."

The sobbing stopped. "You talked to my dad?"

"He's the one we're meeting. He asked me to trust him and said he can get you treated."

Lex looked up at Ethan. "I have to go. My dad will help. I was nervous about leaving too. But I want to fight this. I don't want to lose you or Luke."

"Your dad can really do this?"

"If he said he can, then he will."

He leaned down and kissed his wife, then lovingly dried her eyes with the sleeve of his shirt.

"Okay," Ethan agreed. "But if anything happens to her," his voice began to choke up, "I am holding you responsible."

What else is new, Lilly thought to herself.

"That's not fair," Lex argued.

"Fair or not, I am entrusting my wife in your care."

"I'll be back before sun up," Lilly explained. "We are meeting your father at noon and have a fair distance to travel."

The day was fading fast.. In another hour the sky would begin to darken.

Lilly went through a mental checklist in her head.

> *Lex's treatment…check*
> *Packed for the road trip…check*
> *Phone with scrambler…check*
> *Find Tread*

That was the last thing she needed to do. She headed back to the apartment. The town still sounded eerily silent, almost like a ghost town, except with all the renovations and construction projects Spero looked too new.

If not for her best friend having cancer, the government trying to hunt her down and assassinate her, and her mom being abducted by a lunatic, it could be a beautiful day. The sun was out. There were a few white, fluffy clouds that spotted the sky. A gentle breeze was in the air. It was a rare day for Texas. A perfect fall day, not too hot, and winter hadn't set in yet.

Looking up, Lilly noticed that miles away in the distance dark clouds were rolling towards them. It reminded her of her life. When she thought things were finally working out, some unseen threat always seemed to sneak up on them.

She heard Tread's voice before she even reached the hallway to his apartment. He was talking with Adam. She gave a light tap on the door before entering.

Tread had told her countless times that she needn't knock. But Lilly could never bring herself to just barge right in.

"Can I come in?" Lilly asked, peeking out from behind the door.

"Of course." Her uncle smiled. "Tread was just telling me where you'll go when you leave in a couple of days."

The exhaustion of the past days showed on his face. His eyes were red and bloodshot like his twin's, although Adam seemed to be holding it together better. He was munching on a green apple, so at least he was feeding himself.

"Tomorrow," she corrected gently. "We are leaving tomorrow. Early."

Tread raised a questioning eyebrow.

Lilly filled them both in on Lex's new treatment schedule, the VAS facilities in Little Rock, and about Henry and his scrambler for the phone.

"Well you have been busy." Tread smiled. "No wonder I couldn't find you."

"Did you get things squared away with Vanessa?"

"I did." He nodded. "I was just telling Adam that she has agreed to stay. She is in possession of Steel's sword and Annie is helping to make a new schedule for our ever-thinning group of vampires."

"We'll need a car to take to Little Rock, now that Lex is coming."

"I'll check out our gas supply. We have the big eighteen-wheeler but it might be more prudent to see if we can borrow Vanessa's car. It will definitely get better gas mileage." He reached underneath the table and pulled out Lilly's blue backpack. "It's stocked to the brim, but there's a little space left for anything else you deem essential."

"Thanks."

She had everything laid out on her bed. It would only take her a few seconds to toss it all in.

Tread reached forward and grabbed her hand, pulling Lilly into an embrace. "Don't worry, someday we'll look back on this and it will just be an unpleasant memory."

"I hope so," Lilly said, pulling him down into a kiss.

"Well," Tread began kissing her once more, "I'd better go see about a vehicle. You should take a nap and I'll come get you when it's time to collect Lex."

"I'm not going to fall for that again." Lilly pushed him back and picked up her bag. "I can't afford any delays."

"Lilly, I promise I will wake you up."

"You promised before," she reminded him.

His face looked genuinely hurt. "Lil, I wouldn't risk Lex's treatment."

Adam stepped over to his niece and placed his hand lovingly on her shoulder. "Enough, you two. I'll make sure you get woken."

"You need sleep too," Lilly argued. "When was the last time you slept?"

He laughed. "I'm a doctor. I'm used to running on cat naps. This is nothing compared to the shifts I had to pull as a resident. Besides, I can sleep when you are gone."

"But will you?" she countered.

"Yes, Lilly," he said in a mocking tone as if he were addressing his mother.

Tread waved an exaggerated goodbye and left to hunt down a mode of transportation.

"Uncle Adam?" Lilly began.

"Yes, sweetheart?"

"Will you look after my dad? He's not coping well. I think he may need a sedative or something. I'd try and give him something but he doesn't seem to want anything to do with me." She looked down at the ground. "I don't blame him. This is all my fault."

"No it's not," Adam disagreed. He gently touched her chin and pushed it up until she was looking at him. "What happened was horrible, but it's not your fault. None of this is. If it weren't for you, we would all have died in Harbor Cove. Having Elaine in the hands of that…" tears welled up in his eyes, "well, it's horrible. It's hard to process. But it's not our fault. Do you hear me?"

Lilly nodded.

"Don't worry about my brother. I'll take care of him."

"Thanks." She hugged her uncle. "I love you."

"I love you too," he choked out, still overly emotional. "Now go take that nap, I'll wake you when it's time."

The way things had been going lately, Lilly was really looking forward to a time when her body wouldn't need to sleep anymore. She used to enjoy sleeping, the feeling of waking up refreshed. Not anymore. It seemed like a chore now. Something that just took up precious time that could be used on so many other more important tasks.

She closed her eyes and breathed in the scent on Tread's pillow. Even though he never slept, he did occasionally sit on the bed and read. Every vampire had their own unique scent, but Tread's had a hint of sunshine. He used to smell like sunshine and smoke. However, for some reason the smoke scent had disappeared after they left Harbor Cove and she had never asked him why.

Sleep found her quicker than she imagined. Thinking about Tread and how they met pushed out all the anxiety of today's problems, allowing sleep to find her and overtake her.

A nudge jarred Lilly from her sleep.

"Lil, it's time to go."

There were worse ways to wake up than hearing Tread's velvety voice.

She pulled him close, her eyes still closed, and kissed him. For this one moment it was just her and Tread. Just sixty seconds of pure bliss before the world comes crashing back down on her.

"All right," Lilly said, pushing him back. "I'm up." She jumped out of bed. "I just need two seconds to grab my stuff from my apartment."

She darted out of the room and returned a moment later.

"Let's go."

It was still dark when they got to Lex's apartment building. She was sitting on the steps waiting, a small duffle by her side. Her eyes were red and puffy from crying.

The two friends embraced when Lilly reached the steps. "You'll be back here before you know it," Lilly said, uncertain what the right words were to lift her spirits.

"Let's go. Ethan and I said our goodbyes upstairs. I thought it would be easier." Lex sniffed and slung her bag over her shoulder.

As she took the first step down towards Lilly and Tread, the door opened behind her. Before she could say anything, Ethan ran towards her, grabbed her, and leaned her back and kissed her. It was an epic kiss, like Lilly had seen in the movies. It took Lex's breath away and left her stunned. *Everyone should be kissed like that at least once in their life,* Lilly thought.

"You have so much to fight for," Ethan said. "Don't forget how much I love you."

Before his wife could answer, he dashed back up the stairs and into the apartment.

"Are you sure you can walk after that?" Lilly teased. "You look a little swoony."

Her friend's face turned red as she looked away, trying to hide her expression.

"I can manage," Lex insisted, unable to disguise the happiness in her voice.

They walked in silence toward the northern gate where Vanessa had parked her car. At first glance, there was nothing special about the vehicle, but this particular mode of transportation contained lots of hidden gems. It was a vampire's dream car. On the outside it was just a gray sedan with heavily tinted windows. Vanessa had modified it over the years. It was a hybrid with a solar and gas generator. There were hundreds of mini solar panels on the top that blended in with the color of the car. Human eyes would have to get very close to realize the panels were there.

Although Tread and Lilly had no need for the dark windows, the generator would help them travel much faster. There would be no need to stop for gas, as it ran mainly off of solar power, but Tread added a gallon of gas just for good measure.

After storing their bags carefully in the trunk, Lilly climbed into the backseat with Lex while Tread took the driver's seat.

They were supposed to meet the doctor just outside of Little Rock. The only place Lilly was familiar with was the run-down restaurant where Koyt had met Ryan. She wished now that she had cleaned the mostly eaten bodies up. Hopefully Dr. Crews would not venture inside. It was an old building and Lilly had warned him that it was unsafe and liable to collapse at any time. The plan had been to meet in the parking lot.

Tread parked the car about a mile south of the meeting place. Lilly had promised to come alone, and they didn't want his presence to spook Lex's father.

"Stay out of sight," Lilly reminded him as they approached the restaurant on foot.

"I will." He gave her a quick peck on the cheek. "Give me five minutes before you step out of the tree cover. I'll do a quick loop around the perimeter and make sure it's not a trap." He winked at them and then took off into the trees.

"Lil, you don't happen to have a tissue by chance?"

Lilly turned around to see blood dripping from Lex's nose. She looked around frantically. "No. Sorry."

Her friend used the edge of her shirt to dab at it but it continued to bleed, splattering her shirt in blood.

After a minute of her tilting her head back, the bleeding finally stopped.

"I'm feeling kind of lightheaded," Lex said, wobbling slightly.

"Hopefully it's just from not eating breakfast." Lilly scooped her friend up before she could fall. "I'm bringing you to your dad now. Hopefully he stuck to our terms." *Even though I didn't,* she thought to herself.

With Lex in her arms, Lilly stepped out through the trees. There was a single black sedan in the parking lot.

A man in a fine gray suit stumbled out of the car in a hurry as Lilly got closer.

"What did you do to her?" Dr. Crews yelled, taking a few steps forward before stopping.

Lilly looked down, startled at the accusation, and then realized what he was seeing.

Lex was covered in blood from her bloody nose and too weak to walk. But the doctor was not aware of either of those reasons; he just saw a vampire carrying a bloody body.

He waved a hand and three other men stepped out of the car armed to the nines and pointing guns and weapons Lilly had never seen at her.

"Lex, a little help?" Lilly nudged.

Lex lifted her head with some effort. "Dad, put the guns down. I'm fine. I'm just sick. I had a bloody nose and I don't feel well."

"Forgive me if I'm a little on edge after the attack last night," Dr. Crews said cautiously.

"What attack?" Lilly asked in bewilderment.

"Put the guns down, Dad," Lex insisted. She strained to get out of her friend's arms so Lilly set her down carefully.

Lex stood in front of her friend. "Put them down or I am leaving with Lilly," she said adamantly before fainting.

Lilly dove forward and caught her before Lex could hit the pavement.

"Lex!" Dr. Crews yelled as he sprang forward.

He rushed up and pushed Lilly to the side, checking Lex's pulse and making sure his daughter was still breathing.

"You weren't lying. She really is sick."

"I'm sorry. Can you really help her?"

"Yes." He stood up and looked at his security. "I guess if you wanted to hurt me you have had ample time."

"I don't want to hurt anyone. But please don't freak out. I am also not alone. There is another vampire here. He could have taken out your whole security team but didn't. We don't want to hurt people. We just want to help Lex."

"Okay. I am going to trust you now for the sake of my daughter." He waved his security down, and hesitantly they obeyed.

Lilly scooped up Lex and carried her to the car, laying her gently on the back seat. She had regained consciousness but was still lethargic.

"Thank you." Dr. Crews smiled down at his daughter. "I truly believed I would never see her again. I need to get her to the facility I have set up."

"Before you go, please tell me. What attack were you referring to?"

Lex's father explained how Kansas City was ravaged last night by hundreds of vampires. Only a news crew was spared. Or at least, they were spared long enough for them to broadcast the story.

It has to be Koyt, Lilly thought.

"One more question, what are those strange-looking devices that your entourage pointed at me?"

"That's what I do for the government. I make weapons, among other things, to help combat in the war against vampires. Those are all my newest prototypes." He picked one up. "This one releases a high frequency noise that is debilitating to vampires. It doesn't affect humans because they can't hear as well as you can. This is a new hollow-point machine gun filled with lethal darts," he explained, gesturing to a gun that was slung over the shoulder of one of his men.

"How can it be lethal? Vampires can only be killed by beheading or starving us enough to where we become catatonic."

"Science is proving otherwise. Each dart contains hydrochloric acid. We've learned that if we can pump enough into a vampire, their body isn't able to heal as fast as the acid can burn. Don't get me wrong, it takes a lot of acid. It's not one of our top weapons. It's really only effective once the vampire is already down."

"What would you say to giving me a couple?"

He laughed. "You're not serious. You want me to give you these so you can find a way to defend against them."

"That's actually not a bad idea," Lilly noted. "But no, I actually wasn't thinking about that. I am fighting against the vampire who leads the group that slaughtered that city. And as you can see, I am out-manned and a few fun gadgets might help me to have a fighting chance."

"You really do push the boundaries on trust."

"I brought you Lex. I could probably take the weapons if I wanted—" she began, but at the sight of the doctor's eyes she hurriedly finished the sentence, "but that's just not who I am."

"I can't. I'm sorry, but that's asking too much," Dr. Crews explained. "Will you put Lex's bag in the trunk?" He walked around and opened the back of the car.

As Lilly placed her friend's duffle inside, he nonchalantly took out a black bag and placed it on the ground behind the car, careful to watch the others in the sedan.

"I hope you really are as decent as you appear," he whispered quietly. "I need to get Lex out of here. Good luck. You have my number if you want to check in."

"Thank you, Dr. Crews."

She stood behind the car as it drove off. The minute it was gone Tread was by her side.

"Did you catch all that?" Lilly asked, turning to face him.

He picked up the black bag. "It's got a good haul of something from what I can tell," he said, noting the weight. "I got most of it, except that part at the end. Why did he help you after saying he wouldn't?"

"I guess he decided to trust me, but for some reason he didn't want the other men with him to know. Probably because he works for the government. Maybe they would be okay with rescuing a human but handing over top-secret tech could push some loyalties." Lilly pushed an errant strand of hair behind her ear. "Koyt had to be behind that attack, right?"

"I can't imagine anyone else pulling it off. He's the only vampire I know who's been around long enough to assemble that many vampires together, let alone convince them to attack an entire city. They have basically declared war on the human race."

"Weren't they already at war? I mean the VAS's sole priority is to eliminate our race."

Tread nodded. "True, to a point. The VAS keeps cities safe. But they don't really go out hunting for vampires, unless too many people go missing. This is a direct blow. Most vampires have been content to live in the shadows and stay below the radar and out of trouble. Humanity can't let this stand. They will have to go to war."

"What is it Koyt wants? World domination?"

"When Sage was alive, all he seemed to want was her and a child. He wanted a sunwalker to raise as their own. He scoured the hospitals looking for one, but never found one. He was always crazy. I've only learned how crazy recently. He's a good actor. Great at playing a part. Now it looks like he wants to take control. Whether he will be satisfied with the United States of America, or seek for more, only time will tell. But," he placed his hand on Lilly's shoulder, "the longer it takes us to confront him, the harder it's going to be. We don't want his numbers to get any bigger."

"It's hard to imagine the odds getting any worse, but I agree we can't press what little luck we might have on our side," Lilly sighed.

"Let's go get our stuff, and then I'll take you to Alex's place."

Chapter VI

NEW FRIENDS

The entrance to the hidden vampire city in Little Rock was hidden under a gigantic boulder. Tunnels had been built as security increased, and Lilly was grateful because after Koyt's attack last night the city was on high alert. Every VAS officer and police officer that lived there appeared to be on shift.

Tread moved the rock with ease and Lilly jumped down into the tunnel. He tossed Dr. Crews's duffle down and then joined her. She wondered how they would move the rock back, but before she could ask it was already slid back into place.

Lilly noted a chain drilled into the bottom of the rock. Tread must have pulled it back over the entrance.

The tunnel was made out of cement and looked like it went on for a couple of miles. There was no lighting, but they didn't need any. She followed him down until the path diverged into two different directions. Tread motioned to the left and they continued on their way.

Lilly looked down the path and could see it ended at a set of elevator doors. "This looks a little familiar," she noted, reminded of the first vampire community she had visited in Harbor Cove.

"They all do. Sunlight can be a killer," he laughed.

The down arrow lit up after Lilly pushed it. After only a moment the bell dinged and the door opened.

Lilly froze. Standing inside the elevator was her. The woman looked just like Lilly, except she was blonde.

"Lilly?" Lilly asked.

"I don't go by that name anymore." She tried to push past them but Tread barred her path, keeping her locked in the elevator.

"But you're dead," Lilly said, still not believing that her aunt, and namesake, was standing in front of her.

"Yeah, so are you," she paused, and then added, "Well maybe not yet. I can still hear your heart beating inside of you, but that is generally what happens when you become a vampire. Now if you'll excuse me, I have places to go." She tried to push past Tread again but to no avail.

"Not just yet," Tread said. "We have questions for you and you're not leaving until we get some answers." He stepped inside the elevator and Lilly followed suit. After pushing level 3 he turned back around.

"What are you doing here? And don't say you live here because I know that's not true."

Lilly could tell by her aunt's surprise that was the lie she was going to try and use.

"How do you know I don't live here?" she countered. "You don't live here."

"Each community has a head vamp, and Alex would have told me if you moved in."

"I don't have to answer any of your questions." She crossed her arms defiantly.

Lilly couldn't get over how weird it felt to watch her. It seemed like some Stepford version of herself.

Tread leaned in uncomfortably close. "I'll get answers all the same."

"Adam and Dylan think you're dead," Lilly started. "How could you do that to them? They mourned you. They love you."

Her aunt remained silent.

When the elevator door opened Tread nudged her out.

"Find me Alex," Tread barked at the first person he saw.

"Sure thing, Tread," the man answered, jumping into action.

A few moments later Alex emerged. "What are you still doing here, Phoenix? I thought we already sent you packing. Tell Koyt we're not interested." She turned and looked at Lilly. "How do you have a twin that's not a sunwalker?"

"You're with Koyt?" Tread asked in dismay.

"She's not my twin. Phoenix?" Lilly asked trying out the new name on her tongue. "Phoenix is my aunt."

"Let's take this into my private chambers." Alex motioned, as she noticed the attention they were beginning to draw.

The leader of the Little Rock community led them through several hallways and stopped at an ornately decorated wooden door, full of carved flowers, suns, and little birds.

She pushed open the door and led them into a spacious room full of oversized chairs and a large leather sectional.

"Take a seat," Alex instructed.

Tread pushed a reluctant Phoenix down into one of the chairs.

Lilly took a seat on the edge of the sectional, setting her backpack and duffle beside her, and leaned forward towards her aunt, desperately wanting answers.

Alex plopped down casually into another chair, while Tread stayed standing.

"Now, what's going on? Why do you both look exactly the same?" Alex began.

"I'm not sure. We're related…it's just some weird genetic mutation I guess," Lilly answered, then she turned back to Phoenix. "How could you work with Koyt? He's a psycho. Do you even know what he's done?"

"I owe everything to Koyt. He turned me. He saved me from a lifetime of grief and pain."

Lilly scoffed. "Really, it was that terrible living with two brothers who adored you."

Her aunt's eyes bore into her. "You obviously don't know about my mother."

"I know she loved you and she died. I know losing someone sucks. But most people deal with grief in healthier ways, not by teaming up with a lunatic."

"I didn't do this out of grief." Phoenix gestured to her vampire body. "I wanted to live. That's why I did this."

"So you killed yourself to live?" Lilly asked, confused.

Her aunt shook her head. "Staying human wasn't an option for me. Not if I wanted a life. My mom died of ALS. I got tested and I carried the gene. I was already showing signs. It typically doesn't manifest until much later in life, in the forties or fifties. But I won the genetic lottery." She gave Lilly a double thumbs up. "That's when I started searching for anything that might save me. I watched my mother die from this. It's a horrific disease. It doesn't just kill you, it takes everything away from you—your motor functions, speech, even your dignity.

"Most of my searches online led me to dead ends, but eventually I came across a real vampire. It took some time to convince him to change me. But eventually we made a deal. He turned me into a vampire and I serve him for fifty years."

"Fifty years," Lilly choked.

"That's nothing when you're gifted with eternity."

"So, let me get this straight," Tread began, trying to wrap his head around everything, "Koyt changed you in exchange for fifty years as his slave. You didn't care that he was torturing your brother or that he abducted his wife and is going to turn her into a darkwalker."

Phoenix stood up. "What? What are you talking about? He wouldn't do that to my family. And if he did, then he obviously didn't know they were my family. How would he?"

"Um, I think Lilly is kind of a dead giveaway," Alex interjected. "I mean, he had to know there was at least some connection."

"How do I know you're not lying?" Phoenix asked. "I've never seen any hidden rooms with prisoners."

"You just have to trust us," Tread pushed. "I mean, you two are family. Is the resemblance really not enough?"

"Look, I don't know Lilly from Adam," Phoenix said, putting her hands up defensively. "People lie all the time."

Lilly stood up and unzipped her bag, pulling the phone out. "Fine. You don't believe me, but what about your brothers?"

Phoenix's eyes were wide with horror. "No, I won't talk to them. They'll hate me. They mourned for me."

"Too bad. My mom's life is at stake." Lilly glanced down at the phone and noticed she had forty-four missed calls from Ryan and several texts. She ignored them for the moment and dialed a different number. As it started to ring, she placed the call on speaker mode.

"Lilly?" Henry answered.

"Henry, I need to talk to Dylan or Adam ASAP. It's an emergency."

"Okay, it might take a while to find one of them. Hang on."

"Please, don't do this," Phoenix pleaded.

"You won't really believe it unless you hear it directly from them," Tread explained. "Trust me, I know. Koyt fooled me for years."

"Lil, sweetheart, is everything okay?"

Henry had found Adam.

"Uncle Adam. I'm fine. I just need some help."

"Anything. What can I do?" her uncle asked.

"I have…I have someone here who needs to hear what Koyt did to our family. Just to see that our stories line up and that I didn't make anything up."

"Okay, but that might take a while. He's a monster. I don't even know if there is a word for the kind of evil he is. Can the person hear me?"

Phoenix nodded.

"Yes, go ahead Uncle Adam."

"Well, he started by abducting and torturing my twin brother for seventeen years. Dylan didn't even know he had a daughter until she was grown. Koyt tried to kill him when he feigned rescuing them from the VAS…he did so many horrible things, he almost killed Tread, and the last thing he did was take Elaine. Threatened to turn her into some kind of warped vampire. I really don't understand that," he choked back a sob, "but he's probably torturing her now. Whoever you are, please believe me. Please help us defeat him."

"Thanks," Lilly said, looking at Phoenix, who nodded. "Is Dylan doing better?"

"I've given him a small sedative. It seems to be taking some of the edge off."

"Okay, I gotta go. Be safe."

"You too sweetheart. Love you," Adam said before hanging up the phone.

Phoenix sat back down on the chair. "I can't believe this. I had no idea—you have to believe me."

Tread knelt down in front of her and placed his hand on her knee. "We all know how conniving he can be. Why did Koyt send you here?"

"He's building an army. He wants to overthrow the government and take over. He's been planning it for over a decade. I was sent here to recruit more soldiers."

"Even Koyt's not that crazy." Tread shook his head.

"It sounds right up his alley to me," Alex noted. "I mean, he's always felt far superior to humans. He's old and powerful. If anyone could pull it off, it would be Koyt. He was behind the attack on Kansas City."

"But why not just attack D.C.?" Lilly wondered out loud. "I mean, he seems to have the numbers."

"It's all about the show of power. He wants everyone to know how unstoppable he is. He probably wants to see the humans quake in fear, to know their end is coming and they are helpless to stop it," Tread explained.

Alex looked at Phoenix. "How long do we have?"

Phoenix shrugged. "I don't know. I promise." She stood. "I haven't seen Koyt in months. I've been out recruiting and sending vampires his way. I'm supposed to meet up with him in two days in Jefferson City, Missouri. He keeps a house there. I've been to it a few times. He visits it every couple of years. He has a ki—"

"Maybe we can finally get ahead of him this time," Tread interrupted Lilly's aunt, his face lighting up with an idea. "We're still not anywhere close to being ready to take him on, but Phoenix, if you can find out where Elaine is, we can at least get her to safety. Maybe she's in Missouri."

"No way," she said, scooting back in her chair. "You just said he tortured Dylan for years, tried to kill you, and has committed countless other atrocities. I don't even want to think about what he'd do if I betrayed him," her voice began to quiver. "I'm not going back there. I'm done. Count me out of this mess."

"What a coward," Alex said disgustedly. "This is your family we're talking about."

Phoenix looked away, avoiding eye contact.

Tread waved at Alex to cut it out. "I won't lie to you. Going back will be dangerous. Koyt despises nothing more than someone who betrays his trust. But if you run, that will be the same sin in Koyt's eyes. Abandonment is a betrayal. He will never stop hunting you." Tread spoke the words softly and sincerely. "I never realized the extent of his grasp. He has walked this earth for almost a millennium. He has spies everywhere. He will find you and you'll beg for death before it's over."

They had just turned Phoenix's world upside-down. Lilly felt bad for her. It wasn't an easy thing to handle and her aunt wasn't taking it well. It seemed like her aunt was literally shaking from terror at the thought of the torture that she knew Koyt could and would inflict upon her.

"The way I see it, you have two options. Go back and fight alongside Koyt and hope that after your fifty years are up that your freedom is bestowed upon you. Option two, return as a double agent. Help your family. If you bring back Elaine, Adam and Dylan will forgive you for putting them through hell. You'll have your family again." Lilly stood up and walked over to Tread. She took his hand. "We will kill Koyt. You'll have a life where you aren't constantly having to look over your shoulder."

There was doubt in Phoenix's eyes when she finally looked up. Lilly could tell her words hadn't convinced her.

"How can you promise me that you will defeat him? You said he's been alive almost a thousand years. He has bested you time and time again. What hope do any of us have against him?"

Lilly was hesitant to share their plan with her. Phoenix had been part of Koyt's world for decades. But Lilly's gut was telling her that she was family and could be trusted. Her shock and dismay over what Koyt had done to her family were real. Adam and Dylan were her brothers. She loved them, that much was evident on her face. The risk was worth it. There might not be another way to find her mother. If Lilly had trusted her gut from the beginning and not doubted it, they might not be in the situation they were in now.

"We're not stupid. That's why we aren't just going to follow you and try to kill him in two days." Lilly shook her head. "We won't be ready. But we have these." She knelt down and unzipped the black duffle. It was filled with all manner of weapons. She held one up and hit a button.

The sound it emitted was crippling. Tread fell to the ground. Phoenix and Alex covered their ears and writhed in pain. Lilly was barely able to disengage it through the intensity of pain she was feeling.

It took them all a minute to recover.

Alex glared at Lilly. "Next time let's just explain the new toy and not demonstrate it," she said tersely. "Now I need to go check on everyone." She stormed past Lilly and disappeared into the hallway.

"I'm sorry. I know that was painful. But I wanted you to see that we will be able to stop Koyt. If we can just incapacitate him for a few

seconds."

Her aunt looked like she was beginning to believe it was possible.

"We are going to bring our own army," Lilly continued.

Tread's head snapped up. After hearing how many vampires were now following Koyt, they would have to have reinforcements if there was any hope of getting close to the monster. She hadn't exactly had time to discuss this new strategy with Tread yet.

"We are also going to be raiding two VAS facilities here in Little Rock to better equip ourselves."

Tread raised his eyebrow at her second new revelation.

"My point is, when we do meet Koyt, we'll be ready," Lilly vowed.

"I need time to think about this," Phoenix said, standing up.

"Do you have access to a phone?" Tread asked.

"Not here, but I will if I meet up with Koyt."

Lilly scribbled her number down on a piece of paper and handed it to her. "Destroy it after you memorize it."

Phoenix nodded as she slid the paper into the back pocket of her jeans. "Make sure when you exit this room that you look like you're upset with us and want nothing to do with us. Anyone could be a spy for Koyt," Tread added.

Her aunt opened the door. "You are all fools. Anyone who won't join Koyt's revolution is going to be left out in the cold when the new regime takes over," Phoenix barked as she stormed off in the direction of the elevator.

"Any more surprise revelations for me?" Tread asked as he started to shut the door.

"Nope." Lilly laughed. "I think that about covers it."

A hand grabbed hold of the door and stopped it from being closed. "Well now that I've calmed everyone down, want to tell me exactly what the two of you are doing here?" Alex huffed as she stepped back into her quarters. "I mean, I know it's not for anything good."

"I need to make a phone call first and then we'll fill you in."

Alex looked annoyed. It probably was rude to show up unannounced and then demand that the host wait for answers. But forty-four missed calls wasn't something Lilly thought could be ignored any longer.

Chapter VII

RECONNAISSANCE

"Where have you been?" Ryan asked impatiently.

"I'm sorry. Henry was working on the phone and I didn't realize he must have put it on silent. I just saw all the missed calls and didn't even take the time to read the texts," Lilly explained.

"Have you seen the news? This is Koyt, right? Have you found him yet? Say the word and I will send a squad of F-5's to blow him to smithereens."

Technically she didn't know where Koyt was. Two days from now that was a different story. But her mother might be with him. She couldn't let him bomb the location, as selfish as it was.

"We have a solid lead."

"Leads aren't good enough," Ryan cried out in frustration. "How can you watch what happened and not sound more upset? The photos are horrendous."

"Things have been a little busy here. I only just heard about the attack this morning. I haven't seen anything."

"Go turn it on. Maybe it will help give you some perspective."

Lilly looked around but there were no TVs in this room.

"Can you turn on the news here?" Lilly asked.

Slowly and without trying to hide her annoyance at being kept waiting, Alex opened another door and they filed in after her.

The television on the wall was the biggest Lilly had ever seen. It almost completely covered the wall.

Alex picked up a remote off of a small table and clicked on the TV.

"Oh my gosh," Lilly said covering her mouth and almost dropping the phone, forgetting for a moment it was in her hand.

"I can't watch this," Lilly said.

"You have to—this is what is happening," Ryan said tiredly. "Over a hundred thousand people murdered in the space of a few hours. Kansas City is gone now."

Hearing about the attack and seeing the aftermath were two very different things. It was hard to tell where one dead body ended and another started. The city was literally drenched in blood. Among the bodies were children and women; they didn't discriminate in their genocide.

"Do you see the kind of power and followers he possesses?" Lilly asked, turning her face away from the screen when she could bare to see no more. "Ryan, you have to do more. We have to work together. None of us can finish this on our own."

"Lilly, what can I possibly do?"

"We are planning on raiding two VAS facilities. Clear them out or lighten the security. We need weapons."

"You think I have more power than I do."

"Find a way to get it done. You told me to watch the news. These are your people. Koyt's not going to stop. If anything, it is going to get worse."

"I don't know what I can do. It's a little hard to say "trust the vampires" when I look the way I do," Ryan explained.

"You have to try. Maybe it's time to tell the world the truth about where you really were and what happened during those five years you were abducted. Leaving out the location of course. I am sure you can figure out which parts to emphasize."

"How come whenever I call you upset and wanting to see results, it seems like I'm the one that ends up getting chastised?" he asked, but it must have been a rhetorical question because he went on before Lilly could answer. "I'll try. I don't know how persuasive I will be but give me a couple of days. It's not always easy to get a meeting with all the key players."

"Thanks Ryan."

Lilly hung up the phone.

Alex balked. "I must have heard you wrong." She turned the TV off and tossed the remote on a seat. "I know vampires have excellent hearing, but I must be going deaf because I could swear that you said you were planning on breaking into not one," she waved her finger dramatically, "but two," she raised a second finger, "VAS facilities. Are you insane? Two vampires taking on dozens of guards."

Tread folded his arms and gave Alex a knowing look, just as Lilly could tell Alex was putting two and two together.

"Get out," she said seriously. "You're both insane and I won't have any part of this."

Tread laughed. "You're really going to throw your best friend out and turn your back on him? I highly doubt that."

Alex threw her hands up. "Yes, when he has clearly lost his mind. Come back when you find it." She pointed to the exit.

Lilly was about to interject but stopped herself. Tread knew Alex better than anyone. If there was anyone who could get her to reconsider, it was him.

"Do you really want a psychopath running things? If he takes over the country, who knows what will happen. One minute you're in his good graces and the next…" Tread snapped his fingers. He paused and took a step closer. "I know you're scared," he continued.

"I am not scared," Alex argued.

"Then you're braver than me because a thousand-year-old vampire who really has lost his mind…well, that's enough to make me want to run and hide or lock myself in a room hoping he won't find me."

"I'm not on his bad side," Alex reminded him.

Tread snorted. "Of course you are. After all those years I spent with him, you don't think he knows about you? Do you really think for one second that he wouldn't come after you to punish me?" He placed his hand on her shoulder. "Let's just forget all of that for the moment. I need your help. I am asking you, will you help me?" He gave her one of his most charming smiles.

She shoved him hard. "I don't know why I put up with you. Okay, fine. Like you didn't know the answer already. So, when is this suicide mission?"

"Well first we need to do a little recon, and then I need one more thing from you," Tread stated in his most sincere tone.

"What's that, a million dollars?" Alex asked sarcastically.

"Something much more easily accessible…reinforcements."

"Of course you do. Let's put all my friends' lives at stake too."

"Hopefully Ryan will come through and it won't be as bad as we are imagining," Lilly interposed.

"Just your friends," Tread agreed. "The ones you have known forever and would trust with your life. Who knows if there are any of his goons lying low here?"

The next few days were spent doing recon on the two VAS facilities. They were at complete opposite ends of the city. To Tread's dismay, he would lead one team and Lilly the other. That was the only way they could convince Alex and her friends to team up with them. Each group had to have a sunwalker.

Security was definitely more sparse during the daytime, which they expected. Vampires couldn't attack in the sunlight. Even with the lighter security it was still too much for Tread or Lilly to take on by themselves when a single dart could take them down.

Night security was insane. Each facility had motion detectors that scanned the perimeter nonstop. As far as they could tell, there were at least fifty guards on every night shift and machine guns loaded with tranqs were set to automatically fire hundreds of rounds towards the fences if a motion detector was triggered.

They were working on ideas to shut down the power, but even that would only give them about ten seconds before the backup generators revved into action. Just enough time to breach the fence. And both attacks had to be simultaneous so that neither site had a chance to warn the other.

Each team would consist of four members.

In Lilly's group would be Alex, on Tread's insistence, Bear, and Lewis.

Bear was in his mid-twenties when he was turned. He had short dark hair and must have been military in his human life. He was the biggest guy she had ever seen. He was pushing nearly seven feet tall and his biceps had the circumference of a watermelon.

Even though Tread had assured her that as a sunwalker, she was still stronger than him, Lilly had some serious doubts.

Lewis was the complete opposite. He was a stick. He didn't look like he had any meat on his bones. He was a towering five foot four, but Alex insisted he was one of the best fighters she had ever seen. His hair was an electric blue, the color one might expect to be spiked up like a punk rocker, but he wore it neatly combed and kept short.

Tread's team consisted of three women. The first was a British woman named Eloise. She was tall and slender and smiled a lot. The second woman was named Reesa. She was about the same height as Eloise, maybe a half an inch shorter, but there was a toughness in her. Her stance and the way she held eye contact with you longer than was comfortable made everyone know she was not someone you wanted to mess with. The last member of Tread's team was Van. She didn't look like she could be more than twelve years old, even though the vampires on Lilly's team tried to convince Lilly that she was turned in her twenties. She was dainty and kept her hair in pigtails. She chewed gum nonstop and was constantly blowing and popping bubbles. It was a tad annoying and Lilly was relieved when she had been assigned to Tread's team instead of hers.

Phoenix had never called her. After how much her uncle and father had built their sister up and put her on such a high pedestal, it was a disappointment to see she had chosen to side with Koyt.

How much of their plan had she shared with him?

There were about thirty vampires total that lived in the Little Rock settlement, so they had to be careful in their planning and discussions. Alex's quarters had become their main base of operations. Something Tread's friend was none too thrilled about.

Luckily, most vampires used triple soundproofing when building their personal spaces. With such heightened hearing, it was hard to have any privacy. But each vampires' own quarters was the one place they could go and not have to watch what they were saying. Lilly was surprised none of the vampires had suggested this in Spero. Then again, maybe they had—she hadn't been involved in much of the construction. Tread's night crew had handled most of it.

Lilly was reclining on the sectional in Alex's living room, leaning comfortably against Tread and drinking a blood bag, when her phone rang.

She slid it out of her pocket and Ryan's name flashed on the screen.

"Hey, I'd been beginning to wonder about you."

"I know, sorry. Things have been taking longer to fall in place than I originally anticipated," he lamented.

Lilly could hear the exhaustion in his voice. It was hard for her to tell if he was going to relay good news or bad.

"So?" Lilly asked hopefully, shifting forward with anticipation. She could see Tread was hanging on every word too.

"There is no way to just give everyone the night off. Some might refuse the order if they thought we were siding with vampires. My dad is pulling all the strings he can. If this backfires, he could go to jail for treason at the very least. So no killing tonight. You have to promise me."

"Killing is the last thing we want to do. I promise." She hoped that the two teams of vampires would be true to their word. They had discussed their plan countless times and reiterated the fact that violence wasn't an option. Both teams had agreed, but Lilly had only just met most of these vampires. A lot of blind trust was being given.

"The best I can do is lighten the shift by a few guards—"

"Ryan, that's not good enough. Have you seen these places?" she interrupted.

"I wasn't finished," he continued. "I can also have them called to a fake emergency. This will leave both facilities with a ghost crew. Five or six agents tops."

"Oh," she responded in embarrassment. "That is something."

"Remember, no killing."

"We won't."

She hung up the phone and couldn't wipe the grin off of her face.

"Now as long as Alex comes through on the cutting the electricity, this should be easy," Lilly said.

"When have I not come through?" Alex called from the doorway.

She must have entered mid-phone call and Lilly had been too preoccupied to notice. "Let's make sure we don't let up our guard. No matter how much you plan, things can always surprise you."

"We won't," Tread promised as he got up from the couch. "So, we are on for tonight?"

"Yep. Let's go fill in the others," Alex agreed as she stretched her hand forward and helped Lilly to her feet.

Chapter VIII

VAS

The evening air whipped around them as the storm clouds rolled in. Lightning lit the sky in between crashes of thunder. The teams had decided to breach at one in the morning.

The storm was turning out to be a blessing. When the power was cut, there was a good chance that the few remaining crew members would think it was due to the storm and would not suspect that something devious was about to happen.

Alex's friend was supposed to cut the power exactly at one. They had synchronized their watches just like in the old movies Lex and Lilly used to watch.

Lilly glanced down at her watch. It was a quarter till. At any minute, Ryan's distraction would call the majority of the guards away. Alex was huddled beside her; they were both crouching down behind a large bush. Bear and Lewis were on the opposite side of the compound preparing to breach from a different angle.

"Here they go," Alex whispered as the VAS began to scurry around like ants after their hill has been stepped on.

They watched as officers began to load into a van and drive off.

"Is it just me or did that not look like as many agents as we were hoping for?" Lilly asked.

"I saw about eight soldiers load up. That leaves us with around forty more and now they seem to be on high alert." Alex pointed to the men who were feathering out and getting into defensive positions.

"Well at least there are a few less." Lilly shrugged.

"Are you kidding me? We have to call this off!"

"No, there is no time to call off your friend, and two power outages within a day or two of each other will draw more suspicion. We have to do this now or never. No time to reschedule."

Rain began pouring down in buckets and a huge clap of thunder sounded over their heads.

Lilly glanced down at her watch. "Thirty seconds to go. No turning back now. There's no time to warn Bear and Lewis. If we don't go in, they have no backup. I'm going in. You can do what you want."

The lights suddenly went dark and Lilly hurriedly scaled the fence. She heard a huff beside her and then the fence rattled at her side.

"Here we go," Lilly said as she jumped down into the facility. It was exciting and nerve-wracking all at the same time.

She darted past the automatic machine guns and managed to get two guards tied up before the lights came on.

Tread had given them all zip ties. A brilliant idea, Lilly thought. They were simple to use and hard to get out of.

She turned and saw Alex was working on her second officer when the rest of the facility realized they were under attack.

"It's just tranqs," Lilly called loudly. "Use a body as a shield." Unsure where Bear and Lewis were, she hoped her idea would help them.

Lilly pulled the closest guard in front of her just as the air began to fill with flying darts. Seconds later a siren went off. The rain was helping to impair the humans' vision, causing a fair amount of the darts to miss.

It was too difficult to hold a body in front of her while she zip-tied the next human. She began switching human shields. Once they were hit with a dart, they would fall unconscious and didn't need to be tied up anymore.

Alex and Lilly made their way toward the building, tossing bodies to the side when a new one came into reach. Lilly counted ten VAS members that she had incapacitated.

Just as they were about to breach the main warehouse, a grenade was thrown. It erupted into a loud sound, similar to the gadget that Dr. Crews had given her. She collapsed backward, pulling the soldier she was holding on top of her.

Alex crumpled to the ground and was immediately hit with multiple darts.

Lilly stayed completely still. She wondered how Bear and Lewis were faring. When the sirens were shut off a moment later, she had her answer.

She listened as the VAS officers began to come towards Alex's body. There was no way to know how many guards were still conscious on the other side of the facility, but only four appeared to still be standing here.

"We'll take this one, and you guys get the other one," one of the officers called as he bent down to get Alex's feet.

Speed was the key. She waited until the first two were already carrying her friend before she spun into action. First, she grabbed a gun still holstered in the body that lay on top of her, then she held him up as a shield and began firing. The two officers coming toward her never knew what hit them. The two carrying Alex turned in horror and dropped her body. But the rain was coming down so hard the men weren't sure what direction the threat was coming from. Both were darted before they had time to draw their guns.

She picked up one of the freshly tranquilized victims and made her way deeper into the facility. Bear and Lewis needed her help too. There were aisles and aisles of weaponry, stacked high to the ceiling, concealing her vision. Any row could contain a threat. A movement a few aisles up slowed Lilly's approach. She moved cautiously, gun raised. When she turned the corner, she fired at the same time she was being fired upon.

A second later she was laughing. "Good to see you, Bear."

He had the same idea as Lilly had. Luckily both their shots hit their human shields.

"You got everyone on your side?" Lilly verified.

"Yes. Now what happened to the ghost crew we were promised?"

"I don't know," she answered, turning around and surveying all the weapons. "But let's load up before we have any more surprises."

"I'll go get Lewis and load him and Alex in a van."

Bear turned to go back for his friend.

"Bear, you've been shot," Lilly said, pulling a dart out of his shoulder.

He shrugged. "That explains while I feel a little weird. Guess they forgot to change the dosage to elephant size," he joked.

Having two drivers instead of four cut their haul in half. It wouldn't have mattered a week ago. But the more they watched the news footage from Koyt's attack, the more everyone realized a war was on the horizon. Killing Koyt might not be enough.

Bear loaded one van up completely with darts and tranquilizer guns while Lilly searched through the aisles to see what other toys they had.

She had Bear load a case of sound nukes. Dr. Crews's gadget was superior because the sound lasted as long as she wanted it to, but the sound grenades would still cause a momentary pause in any vampire's course.

As she reached the last aisle, Lilly noticed a metal door to her right. She assumed it was probably for an office or a restroom but decided to check it out just in case.

The door was locked. Lilly gave it a push and it didn't budge. She tried again, exerting all her strength. The door trembled slightly.

"Hey Bear," Lilly called. "Think you can give me a hand with something?"

He was at her side before she could finish her sentence.

"It's locked and heavily reinforced. I can't get it by myself."

He nodded and wedged his shoulder up against the door. They both pushed with all their might and Lilly began to hear the sound of metal breaking. Ever so slowly the door began to open, until finally it fell completely off its hinges.

No wonder why this room was locked. Hanging on the walls were eight weapons, all edged in dragon steel.

"Is this what I think it is?" Bear asked in awe.

"Yes."

"I've never actually seen one." He picked up a spear and before Lilly could warn him, he touched the tip.

"Ow," he said more out of shock than pain. A bright red drop of blood began to roll down his finger. "It's not healing," he said, astonished as his blood continued to drip on the floor.

"It will, it just takes time. You're lucky that's only a tiny cut."

They loaded up the rest of the weapons carefully.

"We'd better hurry. Who knows when reinforcements could arrive," Lilly said as she jumped into the van that contained the dragon steel weapons.

Bear barreled into the other van, almost taking the door off as he tumbled in and took the lead. They were going to an underground garage, similar to the one Tread and Lilly had been in, that would grant them access to the vampire community.

Apparently, this was a private entrance that would lead straight down into Alex's suite. Her chambers must have been a lot grander than Lilly knew, because in all the time they had spent there these past few days, an elevator was nowhere to be seen.

The rain had slowed to a drizzle by the time they reached the rendezvous spot. Tread was already loading boxes into the elevator. When he heard the other vehicle approach, he stopped and made his way toward it.

"Everyone all right?" Tread asked as he opened Lilly's door.

"We all made it. Alex and Lewis are unconscious in the other van with Bear."

She hopped out of the van and went to the back of the vehicle.

"How did your team fare?"

"About the same as you, except we only lost Reesa during the breach."

"Reesa is dead?"

"No," he corrected quickly. "I meant lost as in unable to assist us. She just got hit with a dart."

"Oh, good." Lilly sighed in relief. She opened the doors to the van and lifted the blanket hiding their stockpile. "We did pretty good; how about you?" Lilly smirked.

His eyes widened in amazement. "Not quite that well." He ran a hand through his wavy black hair. "We should pay special attention to these. Dragon steel is enough to tempt any vampire, and I've never seen this many weapons in one location."

He wrapped them back up in the blanket. "Take these down and stow them in Alex's bedroom. I'll finish unloading the rest and meet you there." He kissed her quickly and then went to the other van.

She got a few questioning looks as she carried the bundle to the elevator. Avoiding eye contact, Lilly headed straight for the elevator and rode it down.

It opened into what looked like a storage area. There were shelves filled with books, DVDs, electronics, and rows of clothing.

There were two doors leading out of the dimly lit storage area. Lilly tried the one to her right first. It opened up to a wall. Lilly pushed it, and it pivoted forward, revealing a large bathroom.

This must lead to Alex's room, Lilly thought.

The bathroom was twice the size as Lilly's bedroom in Spero. It had a good-sized hot tub that would comfortably fit five or six people in it. There was a walk-in shower with a dozen different nozzles sure to clean every crack and crevice.

A mirror almost as big as the television in the media room hung on one wall. There were two sinks with a scattering of products lining the counter.

Lilly made her way through the bathroom and into what she hoped was the bedroom. There was no bed, but that didn't necessarily mean anything since Alex never slept.

There was an oversized chair and ottoman against one wall with another large TV on the wall across from it—although this television wasn't anywhere close to the size of the one in the media room. One wall of the room was lined with bookshelves. There was a small table next to the chair and a mini fridge on the other side.

After glancing around the room and not finding any great hiding place, Lilly set the bundle of weapons behind the chair. The spear stuck out the most, but no other option was coming to her mind at present.

Lilly picked up the remote and turned the television on. She wondered if there would be news of their break-in.

Bloody corpses filled the screen. At first Lilly thought they were replaying coverage from the massacre in Kansas City, but as she continued to watch, the horror of what had happened began to sink in.

She turned the volume on and heard a reporter mention St. Louis. This had been a second attack. Koyt was moving closer to Washington D.C.

The attack started around midnight. Now everything made sense. The VAS facility received the news for the false attack from Ryan but knowing they were guarding so many weapons and knowing that the last attack ransacked the whole city, the majority of the men stayed to protect it.

Ryan had probably left her a dozen messages. Her phone was in her backpack in the media room. Not wanting to leave the dragon steel weapons unguarded, Lilly would have to delay the retrieval of her bag. The vice president's son would just have to wait.

The minutes seemed to drag on as Lilly sat there waiting for Tread. She eventually turned the TV off, unable to stomach the images any longer. The door finally opened and Tread walked through carrying Alex in his arms.

Lilly sprung up from the chair to make room for Alex. Tread laid her down gently.

"How long do you think she'll be out for?"

Tread shrugged. "I think everybody is different, body weight and such. When you were hit you were out for a couple of hours," he paused and glanced down at his watch, "So I'd say at least another half an hour."

He put his arms around Lilly and held her close. "I was so worried about you," he explained. "Especially after the guards didn't disperse like we were told." He leaned forward, his lips brushing against hers softly at first and then more fiercely.

She ended the kiss, which was so out of character that Tread seemed to know something was wrong.

"What is it?" he asked, his voice full of concern.

Without answering him, Lilly turned the TV back on and let the images explain for themselves.

"A second one?" Tread asked in disbelief. "When did it happen?"

"Around midnight."

He raised his eyebrow knowingly and nodded. "What'd Ryan say?"

"I haven't talked to him. I left my phone here while we went on the raid. It's in the media room. Do you know where that is from here?"

He laughed lightly. "Yes, I'll go grab it for you." He craned his neck to look behind her. "Um, first off, that's the worst hiding place I have ever seen and second, no one comes in here without Alex's permission. They'll be safe here."

"How should I know?" she called after him as he left the room chuckling to himself. "It's not like there are a lot of options here."

"Do you talk to yourself a lot?"

Lilly spun around to see that Alex was pushing herself into a sitting position.

"How are you feeling?" Lilly asked.

"Hungry," she said as she leaned down, opened the fridge and pulled out a blood bag. "Did everyone make it back okay?" she asked before sinking her fangs into the pouch. Alex glanced up at the TV and started choking, spewing blood everywhere. "There was another attack?" she asked once she regained control over her bodily functions.

"Yes, it happened right before we breached the facility."

Tread rushed into the room, phone in hand. "You have to hear this," he said, thrusting the phone into Lilly's hand.

She took it hesitantly. The look on Tread's face gave her pause to concern, wondering if she really wanted to know.

Chapter IX

RESTLESS

"Ryan," Lilly said calmly, trying to not let her anxiety get the better of her.

"We have less than two weeks. In less than two weeks, Koyt attacks Washington D.C. with his army, unless the government offers a total surrender."

Lilly gasped. "How do you know?" she asked after recovering from the shock of his announcement.

"He sent us a message. It was written in blood and delivered by a senior staffer who claims he was stopped last night on his way home and threatened with his life if he notified anyone about it before this morning."

The date Koyt had given Ryan was the night of the full moon. It wasn't a coincidence the two dates coincided. Koyt had planned it this way. He wanted all of his revenge in one fell swoop.

"We're all going to die," Ryan said, his voice quivering in fear. "If we surrender, we die or become human blood bags, and if we don't, we die an excruciating death."

"We have to stand and fight," Lilly told him determinedly. "Vampires and humans together. We'll take a stand at the White House."

"They'll never go for it."

"They don't have a choice. Bring them to Spero. It's a risk for us too. Let them see that not all vampires are evil. That we can live together peacefully. Let them talk to the humans there. Force it if you have to."

"You want me to abduct the president of the United States?" Ryan asked in a whisper.

"Temporarily, yes. If you have to. Convince your father to help. What other options do we have? It's either to end this or we all die."

"Will you be there?" Ryan asked. "If I can convince them?"

"No. We have two weeks to do our own recruiting. I have an idea or two—I may need you to make a phone call. But first we need the president on our side."

His laugh was slightly hysterical. "Every time I talk to you, I don't think your requests can get any more impossible…but then you surprise me again and again."

The next few days passed in silence. Lilly didn't hear a word from Ryan. Tread and Alex explained to the Little Rock community what was happening and laid out their choices. A few left, whether to run and hide or join Koyt's side, Lilly didn't know.

It wasn't a simple choice. Although most had heard stories over the past year about an ancient vampire that no one wanted to get on his bad side, taking sides now came with a lifestyle choice.

Tread made it clear that if vampires helped to save the United States from Koyt's army, things as they knew it would be changing. They would no longer be allowed to kill humans for blood. Blood bags would be their only option. He explained the freedom that came with it, and some new possibilities like sunlit pathways and getting to be above ground in daytime. This would take time to spread to other cities of course, but it was something to look forward to.

The humans would have to make changes too. Blood donations would have to become mandatory. If the president agreed to their terms, a new world was on the horizon.

Twenty-five vampires remained. Not a lot considering Koyt's army of five hundred.

Bear had been charged with inventorying and arming each of the remaining vampires. He hadn't been happy with Lilly's decision to send half of the supplies to Spero, but knowing Koyt could strike anywhere at any time, Lilly felt a sense of relief knowing her friends and family had more than just a sword to protect them.

Reesa and Lewis had volunteered to deliver them and then decided to stay and help protect the city.

Lilly was going crazy being cooped up underground. She missed the sunlight and the fresh air.

"I've got to get out of here," Lilly notified Alex and Tread. "Even if it's just for an hour. I miss the sun."

"Really?" Alex asked, seeming annoyed. "You miss the sun, poor sunwalker who has had to go a few days without it. How do you think the rest of us feel?"

The relationship between her and Alex seemed to be on a seesaw. Sometimes it was good, but then it would suddenly plummet. To say she had put her foot in her mouth would have been a gross understatement.

"She didn't mean anything by it," Tread said, coming to Lilly's defense. "She's not used to vampires having to hide out underground. Lilly was brought up in a different world than us. Before we moved to Spero, she didn't know other vampires. And now in Spero, well, you've seen the pathways—they let light in, but block the harmful UV rays. She's not used to this."

"Sorry," Lilly added.

"Me too," Alex said. But Lilly wondered if she meant it or if she was just apologizing due to Tread's eyes baring down on her. "I'm just on edge. This whole situation is crazy. I'm arming my friends to face almost certain death."

"We are all in it together," Tread reminded her.

"I'm going to go through the tunnels and back up by the car. I just need some fresh air."

"I'll come with you," Tread offered.

He took her hand and gave a curt nod to Alex as they left.

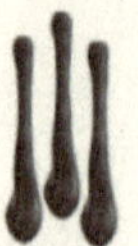

The sunlight was exhilarating. She wasn't certain if vampires could become depression, but she knew the daylight had made her feel a hundred times better.

She took a deep breath and smiled.

"I don't know how you were able to live down there for so long," Lilly commented, stretching her arms over her head.

"It's not exactly a choice for us. Things might be changing, but there weren't a lot of options," he reminded her.

He walked up behind her and rubbed her shoulders. Then he slowly began to kiss her neck and up her jawline as he turned her towards him. He was just brushing his lips against hers when the phone rang.

He sighed. "I'm not sure how much I like that thing," he complained as Lilly pulled it out.

"Hello," Lilly answered. It was Dr. Crews's number. She had called it yesterday and left a message asking him to call her.

"Lilly, it's so great to hear your voice."

The voice on the end of the line sounded tired and weak.

"Lex! How are you feeling?"

"Nauseous all the time. I started the chemo a couple days ago. It sucks." Lex laughed. "But on the bright side, my dad thinks we caught it on time. He said it hasn't been overly aggressive, and his friend, Dr. Quigley, the oncologist, is super nice. Plus he promised me that…," Lilly could tell she was trying to hold back tears, "…my mom is coming to visit tomorrow."

"That's amazing, Lex."

"I know, I just miss Ethan and Luke so much. I think that's actually worse than the chemo, if you can believe it. But there's been a lot of advancements in science. I'm still going to lose my hair probably, but the treatment time is a lot shorter than it was even twenty or thirty years ago. I could be home in a couple of weeks."

"I'm so happy for you, Lex, and for me because I miss you like crazy." Lilly laughed lightly. "Can I talk to your dad?" she asked.

"Um, sure, just give me a sec."

"Just have him call me right back. Love you, Lex."

She hoped ending the call and restarting it would reset her ten minutes. Lilly could tell Lex thought the request to talk to her father was strange, but she didn't want to worry her friend with the chaos going on around the world. All Lex needed to focus on was getting well.

The phone rang a couple of minutes later.

"Dr. Crews?" Lilly verified.

"Yes. Lex said you wanted to talk to me."

"Have you seen the news?"

"You mean the second attack? Of course I've seen it," he said tersely. "I hope you didn't mention that to my daughter."

"Of course not." Lilly was appalled. She had more common sense than that. "I'm going to put my trust in you, doctor. I'm going to trust you because I need your help. And I need this to stay between us. What I am going to tell you can't be repeated. This is where the trust plays out."

"What are you talking about?"

"I don't know if Lex has told you much about where she lives and what has transpired this past year."

"A little," he said.

"Well, one of the human men who lived with us was named Ryan. He had been held prisoner for five years and I helped facilitate his freedom."

"I'm still not following what this has to do with anything."

"His full name is Ryan Silver," Lilly said the name slowly, allowing time for it to sink in.

"You rescued the vice president's son?"

"I did, and believe it or not, we became friends. We have stayed in touch and a couple of days ago he told me something the president is not sharing with the world."

"I'm listening."

"Koyt, the vampire who has been leading these attacks, gave the president an ultimatum. In just over a week, either the president surrenders the country over to him, or Koyt will ascend on the capital with his army and won't stop until everyone is dead."

There was a long pause before Dr. Crews answered. "Can't you just go and stop him? Lex said you're stronger than other vampires because you can walk in the sun."

"He is a sunwalker too and he's a lot stronger than me. Plus, he has too many followers. I want to stop him, but I can't do it alone. Some of your tech is pretty advanced, and I am sure I have not seen it all. I need more, lots more. Everything you have."

"You want me to arm a bunch of vampires with all the weapons I have created to stop them?" he asked in disbelief.

"Pretty much. And you'll be arming humans too. We are going to fight with the president's security and whomever else he can muster up."

"That's asking way too much for me to just go on blind faith," he said.

"I know, just get things ready. Ryan is working on getting the president to agree. They will contact you, hopefully soon, but we need\' to start getting things in motion."

"Just as long as we are clear that I am not handing anything more over unless I hear from the president."

"I'll be in touch," Lilly said before sliding her phone back into her jacket pocket.

Reaching forward, Tread pushed a strand of hair out of her face. "You know," he began, "you're hanging a lot on a guy who hasn't called you back."

"What choice do we have?" She leaned her head down on Tread's chest and sighed. Then she stepped back and looked at him. "Do you really think twenty-five of us can take on five hundred?"

"Probably not, but…" he smiled, "if we take Koyt out, everything might just fall apart. With no sunwalker to lead them, they might not be so brash. Or who knows what he has over them. Look at what he did to Johnny, not to mention the deal he made with Phoenix."

"Perhaps…Or his followers are just as crazy as he is."

Tread shrugged.

The phone chimed and Lilly pulled out her phone. The message was from Ryan.

President thinks it's a trap. Refuses to join sides. Going through with your insane plan. Tell Spero to be ready tomorrow. If I'm not in prison or worse I'll call you when it's over.

"Wow," Lilly exclaimed, showing Tread the text. "I mean, I know I suggested it but Ryan is really going to attempt to abduct the president of the United States. It sounds crazy even to me."

A voice sounded from below in the tunnel. "We have a problem down here. A little help would be nice."

"I'll go," Lilly volunteered, handing Tread the phone. "I need to earn a little goodwill from Alex. I don't think she likes me that much. Call Henry, see if he can find Annie and Adam. They should be the ones to lead the tour. They probably have the best vampire-human relationship outside of Lex and me," she winked, "which will be good for them to see."

Lilly jumped into the tunnel and found Van hugging the shadows. "What's the problem?"

"Alex decided it was time to dole out the dragon steel weapons, and it's not going very well."

Lilly rolled her eyes. There were only eight weapons. Everyone would want one. She wondered how Alex had determined the lucky recipients, and if Tread knew about any of this.

She sped through the tunnels, following Van, and stopped in a large common area. It looked like everyone was in attendance. There was so much arguing going on, it was hard to keep it all straight.

"Enough!" Lilly yelled. "Why are we even doing this now?"

Alex threw up her arms. "Because someone let it slip that we had these weapons and I have twenty-five vampires demanding to know who is going to get one." She glared at the crowd. "I'm trying to determine a fair way to choose."

"Who spilled the beans?" Lilly wondered out loud.

"If I knew that, there would be consequences." Alex glared at Bear, Eloise, and Van. "All of them are claiming their innocence."

The eight weapons were laid out on the table: a spear, a long sword, a saber, two daggers, a mace, an axe, and a double-sided axe.

"So, what have you come up with? Putting numbers in a hat and drawing?" Lilly asked, looking at the desperate group before her.

The odds were not in their favor. She didn't blame any of them for wanting a weapon to defend themselves against Koyt and his army.

"We spar," Tread said, coming up from behind. "It's simple. The best fighters get the best weapons. Those who aren't as skilled at combat get dart guns and weapons that can be used from a distance."

"You were quick," Lilly noted.

He winked at her and then walked over to the table. He picked up the axe and double-sided axe. "These are for me and Lilly, unless one of you thinks you can take us in the ring?"

There was complete silence.

"All right then, if you still want a shot at one of the remaining items here, then follow me to the sparring room."

Lilly helped Alex collect the rest of the weapons and followed the group to a room she had never been in.

There were four boxing rings, each with a scattering of folding chairs around them.

A few vampires decided for whatever reason not to compete. Lilly wasn't sure if they were new vampires, or if they just knew they couldn't stand up against more seasoned fighters.

There were sixteen ready to fight for a dragon steel weapon, including Alex. Lilly thought it seemed a little unfair for Alex to be in the competition as well. His friend had done so much for them and led this community. Alex should have just been given one, but Lilly left it up to Tread. He knew Alex the best and maybe she preferred it like this.

Having the youngest vampires fight each other sounded like the fairest idea to Lilly, but she knew a vampire's age was a highly guarded secret. Instead, Tread randomly drew names. It was a double-elimination competition. The first one to pin their opponent won the match.

Butterflies formed in Lilly's stomach when Bear's name was called. He was the biggest vampire by far, and it seemed so unfair to be paired up against him.

The bout went just as Lilly expected. Bear crushed his opponent—a much smaller man who just didn't have the speed to escape Bear's massive hands—in mere seconds.

Van and Alex sparred. They seemed to have fun with it, but in the end, Alex was the clear winner.

The matches lasted most of the afternoon. By the end, the six winners were Alex, who actually beat Bear in a bout, Bear, Eloise, Timothy, Derek, and Ron. They picked weapons in order of their rankings, so Alex went first. She chose the saber, followed by Bear with the spear, then Eloise took a dagger, Timothy the mace, Derek the long sword, leaving the last dagger for Ron.

Lilly thought about offering her dagger to Van who had been seventh, now that she had an axe, but the small knife in her boot wasn't really hers. It also offered her a sense of comfort, having a concealed weapon that could protect her that no one knew about. She felt a little selfish but not enough to change her mind.

After everyone had stored their weapons, Bear and Tread sparred for a bit. Lilly was amazed at how graceful someone of Bear's size could move, but then again that was one gift of vampirism.

It was late by the time the two boys finally called it quits. Lilly kissed

Tread goodnight and went to find an empty sofa in a room Alex had assigned her to use. There were no beds here. It was weird being the only one in the entire underground community that needed sleep. She felt like she was missing out on things.

She yawned and closed her eyes, hoping tomorrow would bring her closer to reuniting with her mother and better prepared for the ever-looming standoff with Koyt.

Chapter X

STRANGER

A loud knock woke Lilly up. Her body's sluggish response led Lilly to believe that it was either very late or very early. Reluctantly, she pushed herself off the couch and opened the door. A vampire she recognized from the boxing ring was standing there. He was about Lilly's height but a little hefty. She remembered the others calling him Bud.

"What can I do for you, Bud?" she asked through a yawn.

"There is a visitor here requesting to speak with you. He's waiting at the front of the main entrance. No one here knows him so we didn't want to let him in without checking with you."

Lilly wondered if something happened at Spero and if Henry, Sam, or Mark had been sent. But they had a phone, so wouldn't they have just called? Of course if Koyt had attacked, it could have been destroyed. Her mind started racing to the darkest places.

"Did you tell Tread?" she asked, stepping out into the hallway.

He shook his head. "No, he's not here. He left with Alex—they said they'd be back in a few hours."

She glanced up and down the corridor. "Bud, I've never been through the main entrance. Can you show me the way?"

He shrugged and started walking, so Lilly took that as a yes and began to follow him. Bud didn't seem to have any sense of urgency and his slow pace was grating on Lilly's nerves. Something might have happened at home and all she wanted to do was hurry up and see who had come.

She was brought to another elevator.

"All the way to the top," Bud instructed, before turning and heading back in the direction they'd come.

Lilly pushed the up arrow and the elevator door opened immediately. Her anxiety grew as the elevator rose. When she finally reached her destination and the doors opened, all she could see was Bear. He was standing in front of her, blocking her view.

He glanced over his shoulder, gave her a quick nod, and stepped to the side.

Lilly moved forward and looked at the stranger in front of her. The first thought to enter her mind was that everyone in Spero was dead and that Koyt sent this errand boy to deliver the news.

"Who are you and what do you want?"

Bear growled, stepping closer to the visitor. "You don't know him? He said he was your friend."

"A friend," the other vampire said, taking a quick step back. "I said I was a friend. I never said I knew Lilly."

The clarification didn't seem to calm Bear down at all. But Lilly didn't mind.

"I'll repeat my question—who are you and what do you want from me?"

The stranger was cute and didn't look dangerous. He was wearing jeans and a t-shirt. He had brown eyes, short blonde hair, and looked about the same age as Lilly. Although she knew in vampire years, looks could be deceiving.

He kept giving Lilly a weird look, and it was beginning to make her uncomfortable.

"Man, you really do look exactly like her. I'd swear you were her…if it weren't for the hair or the heartbeat." He stuck out his hand. "Sorry, I'm Jimmy."

Lilly made no move to shake it, so he dropped it awkwardly, putting it in his pocket.

"Tough crowd," he said. Then he gave a sheepish smile. "Phoenix sent me."

This statement put Lilly on edge. What if something happened to Phoenix? Maybe Koyt found out about her encounter with them and tortured her, sending back his own spy.

"How are we supposed to know if that's true or not?"

He thought about it for a moment before answering. "Well, I'm here. Which means she told me about you. I know she was supposed to call you, but Koyt has been a little paranoid lately so she hasn't had access to a phone. You can ask me anything about Phoenix, her brothers, her human life. I'm a fountain of information." He smiled.

He certainly seems relaxed and genuine, Lilly thought, *but maybe he's just a good actor.*

"You could have come by that information any manner of ways. Maybe Koyt tortured her or perhaps she decided to stay loyal to Koyt. She has been a vampire for a long time. You might know her and have learned about her, but that doesn't mean she sent you or trusts you."

He shrugged. "I guess not. I can't prove Phoenix decided to side with her family. I can't provide proof that Koyt didn't torture her."

He seemed to cringe when he mentioned torture.

"I can prove that she knows me. After that you'll have to decide for yourself whether to trust me or not."

Reaching into his back pocket he pulled out a wallet. It seemed odd since vampires didn't tend to use money. He handed it to Lilly.

It was brown and leather, lightly faded. Not sure what to expect, she flipped it open. Inside there were pictures tucked into little plastic holders. Lilly flipped through them. Each one was a picture of him and Phoenix. There was no doubt in her mind that they were together.

"I would do anything for her." He took back his wallet and slid it into his pocket. "I'll let you decide. I also know where Elaine is being kept," he shrugged again, "but maybe I'm lying about that, too."

He genuinely looked hurt at her distrust.

"I can tell you love her. But we've been burned before. I want to believe you. But trust takes time." She turned to Bear. "Let him in. I won't take my eyes off him."

Jimmy's eyes lit up and he followed her into the elevator.

"You know I could crush your skull like this," Bear said on the ride down. He snapped his fingers.

Jimmy took a step away from Bear and closer to Lilly.

"Are you sure Koyt's the one we need to look out for?" Jimmy asked, only half joking.

The doors opened and Lilly tugged on his sleeve. "Come on."

Not wanting their new friend to overhear any mention of their upcoming plans, Lilly brought him to her room.

"Maybe I should have given you the conditions before I brought you down here, but here they are," she began when they had entered her room.

"Should I write these down?" he asked in an attempt at humor.

"Number one, if you leave this room without me, you will be terminated on site, no questions asked."

He shifted uncomfortably on the sofa.

"Number two," she continued, "if I find out you're lying about any information you give us, you'll be terminated on the spot. And number three, if you try to leave any time after accepting these terms—"

"I got it—you'll kill me." He put up his hands in surrender. "I will accept the terms, but honestly two and three sound a little redundant. I mean, if I tried to escape, it would obviously be without you and I'd have to leave this room to attempt it."

She picked up a pillow off the floor and hurled it at his face.

It smacked him hard, his reflexes not being as quick as hers.

He laughed and Lilly found it hard not to like Jimmy. He didn't seem dishonest or creepy like Hunter or Koyt did. She didn't get the same uneasy feeling around him as she had the others.

"So, can a guy get something to eat around here or does that end in termination as well?"

She opened a small fridge Tread had moved to her room and tossed him a blood bag.

He looked at it skeptically.

"We don't kill people. When Koyt is dead, that's going to be off the table for all vampires."

"Can we at least pop it in a microwave?" He turned the bag over in his hands, looking at it in disgust.

"Just drink it. I've been told the temperature of the blood doesn't take too long to acclimate."

"So what do you drink?" he asked before sinking his teeth into the bag.

She laughed as he scrunched up his face and quickly drank his meal.

"The same thing as you, but I was raised on the stuff. I've never known any difference."

"Hmm," he said, raising his eyebrows in curiosity.

After making sure Jimmy had his fill of blood, she pulled a folding chair out from the corner of the room. Lilly set it up in front of him and sat down.

"So, let's say I believe everything you told me." She began rubbing the sleep out of her eyes. "Where is my mom?"

"Who is…oh, Elaine is your mom." He scratched his head. "Phoenix forgot to mention that. Man, Koyt really hates your family. I mean, he tortured your father for years, and then he kidnapped your mother. What did you do?"

"I didn't do anything. Besides, it's a long, complicated story and you're not asking the questions, Jimmy. I am."

He leaned back against the cushion and smiled. "You're right. I apologize. You want to know where your mother is. Elaine is being held in Colorado. Denver to be precise."

It took all she had to keep her expression neutral. This could be a lie, but if it wasn't, then they could finally rescue Elaine.

"What condition is she in?"

"That I don't know. I just know that she's not to be touched. Koyt is keeping her in the basement of some house he owns."

"And you could take me to her?" Lilly asked.

"I know the place. I've been there a few times."

"We can leave in the morning. I'll need to get a few things ready."

Jimmy threw his hands up in the air. "Hold up a sec. We can't rescue her yet. The place is being heavily protected, but almost everyone is supposed to be in D.C. in a week. That's when you can rescue her."

"No, we have to go now. He's going to turn her into a darkwalker."

"He can't do that until a full moon," Jimmy assured her. "I won't tell you where the house is or show it to you until then. I never returned from my last recruiting assignment. Everyone is going to know I betrayed Koyt and they'll all be gunning for me."

"So, if Koyt already knows about you, then why didn't Phoenix just run too?"

"Koyt hasn't let her out of his sight. He depends on her a lot and said she was too valuable to send out again, now that the time of the vampires was coming to hand. Look, I know it's cutting it close," Jimmy said sincerely. "Koyt's attack and the full moon fall on the same night. But he will be in D.C. Denver is on the other side of the country.

She can't be changed unless she's bitten under a full moon, so we just have to rescue her earlier in the day."

Waiting until the last minute seemed dangerous to Lilly. Especially if Elaine really wasn't there. They would have wasted all that time in vain.

"I am going to give you two choices. If you want to earn my trust, then you take me to my mom now and prove to me that she's really there. If you're telling me the truth, I'll wait and follow your plan. The second choice would be you refusing to tell me. At which point nothing you say will hold any value. I will go to Denver now and tear up the city searching for my mother, and you will become my prisoner."

"Am I not already your prisoner?" he asked.

"You chose to stay of your own accord and you accepted the terms set forth."

"So I take you, we do recon, and we come back when the place isn't heavily guarded?" he verified.

"Correct."

"Deal." He stuck out his hand and they shook.

"What exactly are we shaking on?" Tread asked from behind Lilly.

"Where have you been?" Lilly said, turning. She had heard him enter as they were agreeing to the terms.

"No deflecting. I asked my question first." He took her in his arms but didn't let his eyes off of Jimmy.

"Jimmy here is going to take me to my mom. But we need to leave now so I can get him into Vanessa's special car before sunrise. What time is it?"

Tread looked at the stranger skeptically.

"No, he's going to take me." Tread handed Lilly the phone. "I forgot to give this back to you. Dr. Crews called. He's requesting your presence. He said he wants to believe you, and he is preparing like you asked. The doc wants you to come take a look at some tech. He's meeting you today. I'll tell you where later. Do you have a problem with that, Jimmy?"

"No, as long as he accepts the same terms." Jimmy smiled.

"We're letting him dictate terms to us?" Tread asked, baffled.

"I set the terms, he agreed," Lilly explained. "Give us a minute Jimmy."

She motioned toward the door, and they stepped outside. Lilly explained Jimmy showing up, the timetable with Elaine, and her gut feeling.

"I just feel like I can trust him." She sighed and leaned against the wall. "I don't know…maybe I'm being naïve, or perhaps I'm just so desperate to find my mom I'm willing to believe anything."

Tread cradled her face in his hands. "If we're going to trust anyone's instincts, it's yours." He leaned down and kissed her—one long kiss and then a quick peck. "I'll go find your mom. If he's right and Koyt has left her heavily protected, we'll come back as agreed upon, but if I see a way to save her now, I'm not waiting."

"I wouldn't want you to. I'm surprised at Dr. Crews's call."

"Honestly, I'm not. I'm sure he's seeing the writing on the wall. These massacres are playing on loop all day long on the news feeds. He has probably realized that humans don't stand a chance without our help." He looked deep into her eyes. "Be careful, nonetheless. We can't afford to get sloppy or let our guard down."

"You too." She pulled him in for another kiss, running her fingers through his hair and bringing him closer. These days any kiss could be their last, and she didn't want to take any chances.

"So," Tread began after kissing her once more, "I'd better get going. Colorado isn't just down the road and I want to be back with plenty of time to get to D.C."

"You never told me where Lex's dad wants to meet."

"Right, I almost forgot." He gave her one of his most charming smiles. "Sorry, you can be a little distracting sometimes. The good doctor wants to meet you on the roof of the hospital here in Little Rock. Just scale the building and be ready to jump onto a nearby roof should the need arise. He wants you there at sunrise, in just over an hour."

"Watch your back. Jimmy hasn't earned our trust yet. He could be leading you into a trap."

"I know. I'll be extra vigilant," he agreed.

Chapter XI

R & D

Watching Tread leave was always hard. She missed him before he was even gone. But this trip was especially difficult. Sending him off on a dangerous mission, with only a stranger to hopefully watch his back, made this unbearable.

Her gut had been right in the past. She tried to remind herself of that fact as they climbed up the tunnel, leaving her behind.

Sunrise was fast approaching. She pulled out a folded map from her back pocket and glanced at the directions one last time. Normally, being in an unfamiliar area, she would have approached Bear, Alex, or another vampire and asked them to show her a location. But today there wasn't time.

Quickly she made her way to the main elevator and rode it to the top. She stepped out into the underground parking garage and made her way to the roof.

With the sun on the horizon, it was safer for her to travel at her fastest speeds by jumping from one rooftop to the next. The city was beginning to wake up. People were on their way to work and taking their morning runs. Whizzing past them at high speeds would not go unnoticed.

She bounded from building to building until she was just two jumps from the hospital.

Trust. Everything boiled down to that one five-letter word. She wanted to trust her friend's father, but history had showed her how much damage a deep-rooted fear in vampires could bring. After all, her father had called the VAS and tried to turn her, her mother, and her uncle in.

She crouched low on the roof and watched as a helicopter landed. Dr. Crews climbed out, keeping his head down to avoid the blades.

Lilly made him wait for fifteen minutes while she scanned the area, looking for any sign of movement. Nothing seemed out of place.

As she jumped across the final two buildings, the thought "a leap of faith" came to mind. She laughed out loud because that's what she was literally doing.

Her impact on landing made a quiet thud. Dr. Crews jumped as she appeared in front of him.

He grabbed his heart. "A little warning would be nice," he yelled over the chopper blades. Are you ready to go?"

Lilly nodded. Even with the noise from the chopper her hearing was excellent. The doctor didn't need to raise his voice. But she didn't say anything. Instead, she just followed him into the helicopter.

It was her first time to fly. It was a thrilling sensation The view was especially neat. Everything on the ground looked so small. Lilly had never been so high before. The chopper flew at a much faster speed than any transportation she had ever ridden in. She wondered if she could run faster than it when it was flying at its top speed.

"We'll be there in a couple of hours. We have to get on a plane from here. It will take us the rest of the way."

Their jaunt to the airport was quick, but the security was heavy. From the way she interacted with the pilots and security staff, Lilly didn't think Dr. Crews had told them that she was a card-carrying vampire.

"Will I get to see Lex on this trip?" Lilly asked when they were both seated and buckled on the plane.

"No, the facilities are not near each other, and stress isn't going to help Lex recover any faster."

The plane was small but luxurious. The seats were wide and made from a very soft leather. There were only four. A nice size television hung from the ceiling. A small fridge and microwave sat on a counter behind them.

Dr. Crews shifted uncomfortably. Lilly could tell he was trying to distract himself, first with a book and then with the television. Hanging out with a vampire was definitely not in his comfort zone.

After an hour he turned the TV off and tried conversation.

"Have you heard anything from the president?"

"I'm not in contact with him, just Ryan."

"…the vice president's son…"

He seemed to be remembering their prior conversation. Lilly didn't think telling him about Ryan's act of treason would help smooth things over, so she kept that tidbit to herself.

"I believe he is going to be touring the community that Lex and I live in today. After that, I expect either you or I will be hearing from him."

"We will be beginning our descent to Harbor Cove in the next few minutes," the captain said over the intercom. "Please remain seated with your seatbelts fastened."

Harbor Cove. Lilly shuddered. Once her home, now it held terrible memories of the price these people had paid for her deception.

"Your facility is in Harbor Cove?"

"One of many, yes. But this site is the testing ground for all of my latest equipment."

The landing was a little bumpy, and Lilly wondered if that was normal. It didn't seem to bother Lex's father.

The captain opened the door to the plane after a small set of rolling steps was brought out. They descended the steps slowly and approached a dark sedan waiting at the bottom.

The day was hazy and overcast. It felt odd to be back in her hometown. She wondered what had become of her home.

Dr. Crews opened the back door, but shut it after Lilly got in. There was a pane of plastic or fiberglass separating the front seats from the back. As Lex's father got into the front, she worried that she had made the biggest mistake of her life. He was a scientist who made weapons that killed vampires and he had just conveniently separated himself from her.

Just as she was going to open the door and travel to the facility on her own accord, a sharp prick pinched her neck. Before she could tell what had hit her, darkness overcame her.

Lilly woke on a white twin bed. She still felt groggy as she glanced around the room. It was odd—the walls were all transparent. Lilly had never seen a room like this before. It took her a few seconds to remember what happened. Dr. Crews.

He had betrayed her. She turned around the room and found the door directly behind her. She tried the handle but it was locked.

She rammed the door with her shoulder but it didn't budge.

What kind of material is this? Lilly wondered.

She went to the far side of the room and rammed the door a second time with all of her momentum behind her. This time the door shuddered.

She could see Dr. Crews running towards her waving his hands at her to stop.

"Wait!" he called. "I'll unlock the door."

Lilly looked around uneasily. Perhaps if she stepped out of the room more darts would come flying. Maybe there was a sharpshooter concealed from her view.

He paused in front of her door and pulled out a set of keys. "Before I open this, just listen to me for a second."

"You just drugged me. I'm done listening."

"It was just a safety precaution," he spit out quickly. "No one is supposed to know where this site is located. I am already taking a huge chance in bringing you here. Please just remember that when I open the door."

As soon as the door was open, Lilly lunged behind the doctor, using him for cover in case any darts came flying. When nothing happened, she slowly stood up, looking around uncertainly.

The room she had been locked in was inside a much larger room. It contained high towers of shelving, each filled with cardboard filing boxes.

"This is where I keep my research notes, as well as the notes of past scientists. If you'll follow me, I'll lead you to my R & D area."

Research and development. That's what Lilly was here for.

"You could have just explained it to me. I could have worn a

blindfold or even pricked myself."

"I wasn't sure that you would trust me enough to allow that," he explained. "I see now my actions probably weren't the best way to gain that trust, but I truly didn't see another option that I thought was viable." He glanced back over his shoulder at the containment room he had kept Lilly in. "I've never had a sunwalker in there before. Guess my room isn't as impenetrable as I thought."

She tried not to think about the other vampires the doctor had put in the room and what had become of them. She had to remember the two species had been at war for decades. Hate had been cultivated for so long on both sides. She couldn't judge him for his past actions, only his current choices.

For a government facility, the building was very quiet. Lilly could hear the hum of the heater but didn't detect any other workers.

They approached a large metal door with a keypad and a scanner.

He placed his hand on the scanner and turned to Lilly.

"Do you mind looking away while I punch in my code?"

"You realize I move fast enough that I could still see it if I wanted to, right?"

"Just humor me," he said tiredly.

Lilly did, and heard a ten-digit code entered in. Then she heard the doctor speak his name and a series of random words into a speaker. When he finished, the door slid open.

As she stepped inside the massive room, she could hear all kinds of noises. There were three workers inside. The room must have soundproofing because even on the doorstep Lilly hadn't heard a peep.

These scientists must have gotten the vampire memo because they all froze when she walked inside.

"It's fine. Just go about your work," Dr. Crews commanded. "We'll be far over here."

He brought Lilly to a table on the far side of the room. Some sort of technology had been laid out on it.

Lilly glanced quickly at the doctor's coworkers. Although they appeared to be busy, their eyes didn't stay on their tasks for more than a second or two at a time.

Not that Lilly blamed them. She and Lex's father were only about a hundred feet away from them. Lilly could be at their throats before they had even realized she had moved, if she had been that kind of vampire.

"This," he began holding up a rubbery looking suit, "is one of my newer inventions. I only have a couple of these and won't have time to make more. This is a new polymer that molds to the body. It's lightweight and impenetrable."

Lilly nodded, not too impressed. She was already pretty much invincible and a suit wasn't going to change that.

The doctor seemed to note her lack of enthusiasm. "Even dragon steel cannot penetrate this."

Her eyes were wide with astonishment. "You're kidding me," she said, taking the suit from Lex's father and examining it intensely. "Can I try it on?"

"Um sure, there's a bathroom through that door." He pointed to a white door in the corner.

Lilly dashed over and was back before Dr. Crews even realized she was gone.

"I still can't get over how fast you can move." He smiled in awe.

"Help!" cried a voice Lilly hadn't noticed.

Behind a table where the three other scientists were working was a smaller glass room. It was closer to the size of a closet than a room. Inside was a vampire, frantically trying to get her attention.

Lilly zoomed over to the glass before anyone had a chance to react.

"Let him out," Lilly demanded.

The three scientists backed up cautiously, while Dr. Crews ran towards her.

"The experiments stop now," Lilly said.

The man behind the glass looked weak and in need of a blood bag.

"You're a vampire, a sunwalker. I didn't realize it until I saw you move." He glanced erratically between the scientists. "Just kill them and let me out."

One of the scientists started digging through a drawer, presumably looking for one of their special weapons.

"No one's going to kill anyone." She looked at Dr. Crews. "This has to stop."

"Lilly, I wouldn't have any of these inventions if we didn't experiment. We even have human test subjects sometimes," he explained.

"But those humans volunteer to do this, and probably get paid for it, right?"

"Well yes, but…"

"This ends now. Vampires and humans need to have equal rights."

The doctor sighed. "I know that's what you hope for, but we are a long way from that."

"Not as long as you might think, Dr. Crews. Now release him before I lock all of you up. And honey," Lilly said to the scientist reaching for a desk drawer, "no matter how fast you are, I'm faster. Plus, I'm now wearing this impenetrable suit. Thank you for that."

"I trust this goes both ways. Equal rights and all. You won't let him kill us."

"Of course not."

He reluctantly handed her his keys. "It's the blue one."

Lilly turned to the prisoner. "I am going to let you out. No one is going to hurt you. Don't try to run and don't attack these people. Remember, I am a sunwalker. This will end badly if you don't play by the rules."

He nodded. "I don't think I have the strength to do anything as it is." He smiled weakly.

Lilly turned the key, unlocking the deadbolt and then opened the door.

The man stepped out hesitantly.

"What's your name?" she asked.

"Kenneth, and thank you." He slid down to a sitting position. "My apologies, I'm not sure how long I've been here and I haven't fed since before my imprisonment."

He looked older than most vampires. Lilly guessed he was probably mid to late forties. Kenneth was dark-haired but just beginning to gray around the edges. He was handsome for an older man and seemed so calm for someone having been through a trauma like this.

"Well that's going to change now." Lilly turned to the doctors. "Who's going to volunteer?"

"To be fed on?" Dr. Crews asked.

"Of course not. To donate some blood."

The other scientists seemed to relax slightly at Lilly's words.

"I'm sure with all your experiments you can hook up a makeshift blood draw." Lilly glared at Lex's father.

"Fine, I'll do it." He went to a cupboard and pulled out the necessary equipment. Then he asked one of his coworkers, Dr. Fletcher, to assist him.

After filling two blood bags, Dr. Fletcher stopped. "If he needs more than this, we'll need to switch places," she said as she pressed some gauze down on Lex's dad's arm and pulled out the needle.

"Let's try these and I'll let you know."

Lilly handed the first bag to Kenneth. He sunk his fangs into it and closed his eyes. He sipped slowly, enjoying every ounce. When he finished, he reached for the second.

"This is so good. Thank you."

Dr. Crews squirmed uncomfortably.

"How are you feeling? Do you need anymore?"

"I could probably down a couple more…but it took the edge off, so I can hold off for a while."

"Kenneth, I'm kind of on a time crunch. You seem pretty chill but I have to make sure everyone stays safe. I'm in the middle of some business with Dr. Crews," she explained. "Do you mind coming over there with us while I conclude it?"

He shrugged. "I'll go anywhere with you as long as it's not back in that cage."

Lilly reached down and helped pull Kenneth to his feet. His clothes were filthy but he looked a lot better after downing two blood bags.

"Doc, do you have any clothes here? He could use a fresh change of clothes."

Reluctantly Dr. Crews left R & D and came back with a pair of light blue scrubs.

Kenneth took the clothes and headed to clean up in the bathroom.

"Let's finish this. I need to get back to Little Rock."

Dr. Crews finished going through the rest of his tech.

"Just load me up," Lilly said. "Get it all ready. We'll need to arm humans and vampires before this is over. And all this is new tech, correct? It's not out there anywhere else?"

"Correct. All this has been tested, but we just started mass producing most of this so it will be new to any VAS officer."

"Great." Lilly smiled. "If you'll just get me back to the plane, I'll call Ryan when I get back. Shipping everything to D.C. will be faster."

"As soon as I hear from the White House," he agreed. "You'll take Kenneth with you?" he asked uneasily.

"Yes. But this time no drugs. You can cover our heads if that eases your mind some, but I won't be knocked out. I think I've proven by now I can be trusted."

"Fine," he answered reluctantly. "Let's get you home."

Little Rock wasn't home, but it was close enough for now.

Chapter XII

DEMANDS

Sunlight. She had left Little Rock at dawn, flown a few hours, and spent a couple more in this secret testing site. Lilly was ready to get home, but she hadn't counted on Kenneth and in all of her haste one tiny detail slipped her mind. Kenneth was a nightwalker. There were still at least a couple more hours left of daylight. So for now, she was stuck.

"So, you've showed me your vetted products," Lilly noted, looking over her shoulder at Dr. Fletcher and the two scientists she hadn't been introduced to. "What are you currently working on?"

He ran a hand along the edge of the table. "Our newest project is a synthetic blood. If we get the formula right, vampires wouldn't need to feed off of humans anymore or," he added somewhat bitterly, "force them to donate blood."

"I'm sorry about that, but he was starving, and it was due to your neglect."

He glanced down at the little bandage on his arm. "This," he scoffed, "is not what I am referring to. I am talking about the track marks in both of my daughter's arms. She looks like a drug addict!"

"I have never forced her to give blood," Lilly said defensively. "However, there are certain requirements to live in a co-species environment. But everyone has been given a choice. They are free to leave at any time."

"Well, this will stop that from being necessary."

"Why don't you tell her what it was really designed for?" Kenneth interjected.

"What does he mean?" Lilly asked, glancing between the two.

"This is a site for weapons R & D," he began uncomfortably. "But that doesn't mean that purposes can't be changed *if,*" he was careful to say if, "the world changes."

"So what was the original purpose?" Lilly pressed.

"A synthetic blood isn't just beneficial to vampires. If we get the formula right, it can be used in human surgeries as well."

Lilly stared at him impatiently.

"But," he continued, "we originally thought that perhaps we could find a way to lace the blood with a latent poison. Inject it in humans and when a vampire tried to feed, it would kill the vampire."

Lilly looked horrified.

"Of course," he went on, "it has never worked. Our human subjects' bodies have rejected the synthetic blood thus far. But we are getting closer. The time between rejections is growing."

"I think it's a great project if it's used for the right purpose."

"Of course, I'll need test subjects when it's ready," the doctor added slyly.

"And we will find you some. *Voluntary* ones." She made sure to emphasize the word voluntary.

By the time the sun had finally set, Lilly felt like the humans were ready for them to leave as much as she was anxious to get home.

Dr. Crews would start loading trucks with all the new tech so that it would be ready to leave at a moment's notice. The only thing Lilly was taking back at the present were the three impenetrable suits.

Lex's father wasn't exactly pleased with the idea of her taking them before he heard from the president, but he resigned himself to the fact after several minutes of debate.

Anything that could protect Tread and keep him from getting injured like before was not leaving her sight. Her only regret was that he didn't have it now on his dangerous trip.

The most pressing concern on her mind at the moment was Ryan's trip to Spero. Not a hundred percent sure of Dr. Crews's intentions, Lilly had decided to leave the phone with Alex. So she had no way of knowing if he had reached out and tried to contact her yet.

Having a bag placed over her head was not a pleasant experience. Especially while riding in the back of a vehicle that she had already been drugged in. Kenneth didn't seem to mind anything. He was just so happy to be leaving Dr. Crews's little shop of horrors. Lilly was curious to know what exactly they did to him but thought it poor taste to ask. Maybe someday if they became friends, she would broach the subject.

When the bag had finally been removed from over her head and they were back at the airport, Lilly promised herself she would never have this particular experience again.

"I'm sorry," the doctor said as they boarded the plane. At first, Lilly thought he was addressing her but realized he was talking to Kenneth. "I'm sure it doesn't mean much, but I am beginning to see some vampires are just the same as humans. I'm sorry for my part in your confinement."

What a nice synonym for torture, Lilly thought.

Kenneth graciously shook the doctor's hand but said nothing else.

The plane ride back was anything but quiet. Kenneth peppered her with questions. It seemed he had been locked up for just over three weeks.

"I still can't believe I'm on a plane with the infamous Lilly Marsh. You've really been hiding out in a city where vampires and humans live together?" He leaned back in his chair and closed his eyes, shaking his head. He opened his eyes. "That's something I don't think I will truly believe until I see it. And all the vampires just drink from blood bags, and they're okay with it?"

"Yep." Lilly smiled. "It takes some getting used to, but there are benefits for the humans as well as the vampires." She leaned forward. "The world is changing, probably sooner than many would like it to."

"What do you mean?" he asked, his interest piqued.

"I'll tell you more when we get back to Little Rock. I need to have a conversation with someone first."

"Ryan?" Kenneth guessed.

She had mentioned the name a few times to Dr. Crews, forgetting there was another vampire in the room.

"Yes, I'll explain it all later. Let's just get you settled first. Besides, we should be landing soon and it's not a short story."

"Fair enough."

Lilly declined the helicopter ride. She knew where they were now and assured Kenneth that they would be faster on foot.

The moon was bright in the sky and reminded Lilly of her ever-looming deadline. She had to reduce her speed a few times to assure that her new companion could keep up.

She led him to the main entrance since it was the most secure. She had learned that the other entrances were only shared once you had gained the community's trust as there was no security tied to them.

Lilly pressed the down arrow. She had only learned recently that it scanned your fingerprint. If you were not in the system, access was not granted and a signal was sent to Bear. That was how Bear knew about Jimmy.

Never having scanned her finger before, Lilly was curious as to how they had added her but hadn't had the chance to ask.

The door dinged and they stepped inside.

"Everyone here is a little on edge, so it might take some time before they warm up to you," Lilly explained.

"Right now, I am just glad to be free." He paused for a moment. Lilly could tell he wanted to say more so she waited. "I hate to ask you for anything more after you just liberated me, but I'm still kind of hungry."

"Don't worry, that I can easily remedy."

She led him down a hallway in the direction of Alex's quarters. Mainly because she wanted her phone, and secondly to introduce Kenneth to the leader of the Little Rock community and get the okay for him to be assigned a room.

They walked past the rec room, a large area with pool tables, ping pong, and foosball. Lilly could hear a new game of pool being started as the balls were racked. She didn't bother looking to see who was playing. Her mind was focused on her phone.

"Kenny? Is that you?" a voice called from the room.

Lilly turned to see Bear coming towards them

"Bear?" Kenneth called out, equally stunned.

They shook hands and embraced each other, patting each other on the backs.

"What are you doing here?" Bear asked. "What's it been, a decade or two?"

"Closer to two, I think." Kenneth laughed.

Bear looked at Lilly. "How did you two end up together?"

"It's a long story." Lilly gave a half smile. "I need to go check on a few things. Do you think you can get Kenneth some blood and then make sure to square away his staying here with Alex?"

"Sure thing." Bear nodded. "Follow me, buddy."

Once Kenneth was handed off, Lilly made her way quickly to Alex's rooms.

She opened the door and called out to see if Alex was home.

"Back here!"

Lilly made her way toward the voice. Alex was in the media room talking with Van.

"I thought you'd be back hours ago," Alex said when Lilly arrived.

"I was delayed. I'll catch you up later. Where's my phone? Did Ryan call?"

"It's over there. I plugged it in because the battery was getting low." She motioned behind her without looking. "And to answer your question, he did call, but he wasn't forthcoming with any information. Said he'd only talk to you."

"Okay, I'll call him now."

"Lilly, I've been around a while," Alex began, finally looking up from her paperwork. "It didn't sound like good news."

That wasn't what Lilly wanted to hear. She nodded, picked up the phone, and walked into Alex's bedroom where it was quieter. She didn't want to be distracted by whatever Alex and Van were working on.

After sitting on the edge of the chair, Lilly dialed Ryan.

"Lilly," Ryan said, answering the phone after only one ring. "It's terrible. The president's dead."

"What? How?"

"It was our helicopter, it crashed. I don't know what happened." Ryan's voice trembled. "We think the pilot had a heart attack. My dad was a pilot years ago, so he managed to soften the impact, but we still hit hard. A piece of metal went straight through the president's heart."

"How are you and your father?"

"We survived. My father broke his arm. Adam said I have a concussion." He lowered his voice to a whisper. "I abducted the president and now he's dead. It's all my fault."

"No Ryan, it was a horrible accident. Does anyone know you took the president?"

"No, just my father. He didn't realize what I was doing. The pilot was a friend of mine. I told them we were going to take a quick trip to survey our defenses in D.C."

"Then there's nothing to worry about. No one needs to know. You were doing what was right for the country."

"It doesn't matter. He'd still be alive if it weren't for me." He was almost crying.

"Ryan, we have very little time before Koyt attacks the White House. I know it's not how we planned it, but your father is now the President of the United States. We need to get him and you back to D.C. ASAP. I have been trying to arm our small band of vampires. We need to meet and work with the human security forces, but no one will come with me if we don't have a treaty or amendments to the constitution."

"Then you need to come to D.C. with me. Make your terms to my father and to congress. At least my dad saw how well Annie and Adam work together. He missed the tour."

Lilly paused, thinking about what Ryan was proposing. "How would I get there?" she finally asked. "I mean, D.C. is the most secure city in the United States. How will I get in?"

"My father will have to call and get us a ride, then we can pick you up."

"A ride? Ryan, they can't know where Spero is."

"It's a little late for that now. My father knows where it is. We'll just have to hope you two can come to an agreement."

"Fine," Lilly relented. "I guess this is what we've been hoping for. I'll meet you on the top of the hospital in Little Rock. There's a flat roof with plenty of room to land a chopper. Just text me fifteen minutes out."

"It won't be until tomorrow. My father's asleep now and needs the rest."

She hung up the phone and sat there quietly. It was a hard decision to leave, more difficult than she had thought. It would mean she wouldn't be in Little Rock when Tread returned.

Her only consolation was that Ryan had a phone. She'd leave hers here with Alex so at least they could communicate. She wished there was a way to know how Tread was doing. To know if she was right for trusting Jimmy.

Lilly was exhausted. The days were beginning to blur together. All she wanted was to go back to her room and crawl onto her sofa. But since Ryan might text at any time in the morning, she needed to have a discussion with Alex.

Tiredly she headed back into the media room. Van had left and Alex was folding up some papers.

"So, what's the news with your secret boyfriend?" Alex laughed.

"He's just cautious."

Lilly filled Alex in on her discussion with the vice president's son and her plans to leave. Then they spent the next few hours discussing the demands that Lilly should argue for. At the end they were satisfied with their list. It was fair but decisive, leaving very little wiggle room.

It would be hard for the president to agree to the terms, but the alternative would be disastrous.

With the list tucked away in her pocket, and Alex apprised of her plans, Lilly fell into bed and let all her worries fade away.

Chapter XIII

THE WHITE HOUSE

A vibration on her end table woke Lilly. She grabbed the phone and saw a message from Ryan. They'd arrive in Little Rock at ten that morning.

It was nine o'clock. She took a blood bag from the fridge and downed it quickly. Alex was a similar build and had loaned her some clothes during her extended stay.

Lilly rummaged through the stack of clothes neatly piled in the corner and grabbed a fresh pair of jeans and a t-shirt before hitting the shower.

There was something about hot water, maybe it was the steam, that made Lilly feel extra clean. The temperature would have been just as comfortable with cold water, but hot was always her preference. Lilly lathered up a generous amount of shampoo and massaged it into her scalp.

She finished showering and changed into the clothing she had picked out. For a second, she thought about asking Alex for something a little nicer. In a half hour she would be meeting the President of the United States, or at least he would be once he was sworn in.

Her backpack was leaning against the wall in the corner of the room. Henry's nifty invention hadn't been put to use yet. She threw a few blood bags inside and clicked the refrigeration unit on, then tossed in a change of clothing, her cool new suit from Dr. Crews, and a few personal hygiene items.

Two dragon steel axes were sitting in the corner of the room. Tread would have to bring them with him. She wasn't sure how well it would go over to try to board the chopper with one of those in hand.

She sat down and pulled on the boots. Her dagger was a different story. It was small and easily concealed. She slid it into her boot and felt the reassuring weight of it resting against her leg. Then she jotted a quick note to Tread.

After glancing over her little one-bedroom apartment, Lilly double-checked her phone once more for messages, left it on her end table for Alex, and headed towards the hospital.

She could hear a few voices in distant common areas as she made her way to the elevator but didn't bother to stop and say goodbye to any of them.

An early cold front must have come through. She could see her breath when she exited the parking garage. It was later in the morning than when she met Dr. Crews on the hospital roof. People were out in greater numbers. It required a little more finesse to cross the building rooftops without being detected.

This morning she landed on the roof before the chopper. She trusted Ryan, so there was no need to do reconnaissance beforehand like she had with Dr. Crews. The helicopter was barely visible in the distance. Technology had come far in some ways. Lilly remembered in the old movies she had watched growing up that helicopters were only used for short distances. Now they could fly across the country on a single tank of gas.

The wind from the chopper picked up a few pieces of trash and blew them in Lilly's direction. She ducked easily and hurried to board the chopper.

Ryan opened the door and slid over to make room for her. He had a nasty gash just above his right eyebrow that had required a significant amount of stitches. He had a few other less severe cuts and bruises, but from the way he moved Lilly could tell he was in quite a bit of pain.

Across from her sat the president. His arm was splinted and in a makeshift sling. A purple bruise adorned his left cheek, but as far as outward appearances, he had fared much better than his son.

As the helicopter rose, Ryan began introductions.

"Lilly, this is my father, President Silver," he said. "He was officially sworn in about an hour ago." Ryan motioned to four men in suits who sat behind them. They had headphones on but were staring at her curiously.

"My dad insisted they wear noise-canceling headphones for this leg of the flight to give us some privacy to discuss sensitive matters. When we land, a press conference will be held officially telling the world about the former president's accident and naming my father as the current POTUS."

The chopper that flew the president was more luxurious than the one Dr. Crews had access to. There must have been soundproofing in the craft's interior because Ryan could converse at a normal tone and everyone could hear him.

Dr. Crews had to raise his voice significantly if he hoped to be heard over the loud noise of the helicopter's blades.

"Between my son and Dr. Marsh, I've had my ear talked off about you."

It was weird to hear her uncle referred to as Dr. Marsh. She hadn't heard that name since they had left Harbor Cove. In their little city, formalities and titles had been dropped. Everyone just called her uncle by his name, Adam. She wondered if he missed the distinguished title of doctor.

"It's an honor to meet you, sir," Lilly responded. "I'm sorry about the circumstances."

"So, tell me Lilly, how do you plan on stopping Koyt? Is your army bigger than his?" the president asked. He reached for a bottle of water and Ryan grabbed it first, opened it, and returned it to his father.

"I don't have an army," Lilly began. "I have a small handful of vampires willing to fight if we can agree on some changes."

"So you'll just sit by and let a whole city be slaughtered if we don't cow down to your demands." He leaned forward. "Tell me young lady, how does that make you any different from Koyt?"

Lilly was taken aback at the statement, and Ryan must have been too.

"Dad!" he exclaimed.

The president held up a hand for his son to be silent and waited for an answer.

"Koyt will slaughter you whether you surrender or not. One way or another you'll end up dead. I will stand by your side and fight regardless of what kind of deal we make. But I will just end up dying in the process if you don't make a deal with us. I have no chance of defeating Koyt on my own. We're not holding you ransom. The vampires I associate with are not threatening to harm you. You have hunted them down and killed their friends. Yet they are still willing to come to your aid if change is on the table.

"Our chances of winning are not great. But I believe if we stand side by side with your soldiers and arm ourselves with a few surprises that we stand a chance. But the other vampires won't fight for free like I will. My hatred for Koyt runs deep. Other vampires won't risk putting themselves on Koyt's radar for nothing. All the vampires are asking for, the ones willing to risk their lives for your people, is equality."

"Equality? We can never be equal. You could crush us in an instant." The president shook his head.

"And France could drop a nuclear bomb on the United States and crush it. We all have power to hurt each other, but I believe with changes in laws and policies that it's possible."

"What exactly are you looking for?"

"We want freedom. Freedom to not have to constantly look over our shoulders, the same freedom you will get in return. We register ourselves, agree to abide by the laws, and get the same rights as every citizen. We build jails capable of housing rogue vampires, just like you have for humans who disregard the law."

"And what about feeding?" the president asked.

"Blood donations become mandatory." Lilly was used to the horrifying expression that followed.

"No, I can't force people to do that."

"Isn't it better than the alternative? Besides, it won't be forever. You have a scientist on your payroll that has been working on a synthetic blood. He assures me he is close."

The president rubbed his face tiredly. "You certainly appear to be well informed." He glared at Ryan.

"It didn't come from me," he promised. "This is the first I'm hearing about it."

"Is there anything else in these absurd demands that I need to think about?"

"Pardons. We all want pardons for any past wrongs. Also, we want a seat at the table."

"What does that mean?"

"We need representation in Congress and on your staff."

"Are you crazy? Why would I ever agree to that?" he balked. "How would I get Congress to agree to that? We are on shaky ground here. Emotions are running high and I need to prove to the people and Washington that I am stable enough to be the new leader of this country. They could easily invoke the twenty-fifth amendment if Congress believes I've gone off the deep end and handed the reigns of our country to vampires. It will be difficult enough to convince them to allow vampires to assist us, let alone give them political power."

"I've heard you can be pretty convincing. You asked why you should agree—I'll tell you," Lilly began. "First, to help establish a sense of trust. The people of the United States need to see we can be trusted and that not all vampires are bad. We want two seats and a position on your staff. As well as a few spots on the VAS, which will be renamed and will focus on hunting down all criminals and protecting both species."

"Are you hearing this?" he asked his son. "I thought you said she was sensible."

"I think I said she was going to shake things up."

Lilly pulled a folded piece of paper out of her pocket and handed it to the president.

"I've written them down. Take some time to really think about it. We will hold you to your agreement. But remember, time is ticking away."

He huffed but took the paper and placed it in his pocket.

The rest of the trip was pretty quiet. Lilly and Ryan chitchatted about the few people he had seen in Spero. She wondered what the president was thinking about.

The requests she asked for might be hard to implement and difficult for the general public to accept at first. But it only seemed fair for the vampires to have equal rights, especially when they would be risking their lives to fight for this country.

No matter the outcome, there would be losses on their side, both vampires and humans. Koyt's army would not leave them unscathed, even if they did manage to pull off a victory.

When the helicopter landed, secret service agents descended upon Ryan's father, whisking him away, most likely to a press conference to introduce him as the new president.

"So how about a tour?" Ryan asked, offering her his arm.

"Sounds like a plan. We need to find all the weak points in your defenses," she answered, sliding her arm through his.

"I guess that means we should start outside."

The gardens were gorgeous. There were rows and rows of flowers and exquisitely carved statues. Some of the bushes were even carved into intricate designs. A few fountains were spread out along the beautiful slate paths. Lilly was glad that she was able to see the gardens now. In a few days, she imagined there would be nothing left.

The perimeter was much longer than Lilly had pictured. There were almost innumerable entrance points. The wall surrounding the capital was at least fifteen feet high and had electric current running through it. There were guard towers with VAS snipers every fifty feet. A few vampires wouldn't stand a chance. They would be gunned down as soon as they reacted to the electric current.

But the horde that was traveling with Koyt could easily overwhelm the wall and knock out the electric current. Sure, the snipers would be able to hit a few vampires, but not nearly enough.

There were large speakers attached to several of the guard posts.

"Ryan, what are those for?" Lilly asked, pointing to one of the towers with the speakers.

"The grounds are large. Occasionally we make announcements over the PA system. It's the quickest way to get information out to everyone at once."

It felt strange to be followed everywhere she went. Lilly hadn't realized that Ryan's security detail followed him nonstop. Of course it made sense now. He had called her before hiding out in the bathroom.

As they turned to walk inside, she whispered, "Does anyone here know what I am?"

He shook his head. "No, not yet. But after my father makes his decision, if he needs the support of Congress, everyone will know."

As they walked through the various rooms, Lilly was surprised at how many people worked at the White House.

"You really should start to evacuate all non-essential personnel, as well as the civilian population. The more bodies here, the higher the death toll will be."

"I'll bring it up with my father."

Ryan was just showing her the Lincoln bedroom when someone began shouting.

"Vampire! Shoot her!"

Everyone in the vicinity began looking around, confused as to where the threat was coming from. An officer drew his gun and aimed towards Lilly, firing several times.

She moved swiftly, avoiding the darts.

"Stop!" Ryan yelled.

But the VAS officer ignored him and continued firing.

Knowing the darts were coming, it was easy for her to avoid them, but now other officers were beginning to draw their weapons. Soon there would be too many for her to be able to dodge them all.

Ryan kept yelling. "Stop! Get behind me, Lilly. I order you to stop!"

The soldiers stopped shooting but kept their guns pointed at Lilly, who was now behind Ryan. They continued to inch their way closer and closer.

"What in the world is going on here?" President Silver asked, coming out from behind a door hidden in the wall. "Holster your weapons," he ordered.

"But sir, she's a vampire. I recognize her from the news."

"That she is," the president acknowledged, "and she is here as my guest, and you will treat her as such."

The stunned looks on the soldiers' faces were priceless. But they still looked back and forth between the president and Lilly uncertainly.

"I'll have you court-martialed and charged with disobeying a direct order if you do not holster those weapons immediately."

Power rang from Ryan's dad's voice. It didn't take him long to seem presidential.

The officers finally, one by one, began to lower their weapons.

"If you'll both come with me," President Silver said, holding the door he had just emerged from open.

Quickly and gratefully Lilly slid through into the next room with Ryan at her heels.

The president entered last, closing the door behind him.

"Well now, my apologies for that. I didn't think the staff would recognize you and I thought it might be easier for them to believe you were human for the time being." He scratched his chin. "I guess this pushes my decision deadline up. If I don't explain what I'm doing letting a vampire roam through these halls, some might begin to see me unfit to run the country."

"This is the only way we stand a chance, Dad."

"It won't be easy. I might easily become the most hated president of all time, but I don't see any other way out of this situation. If we want the United States to still be around in a few days from now, this is our only chance. I'll have the paperwork drawn up a bit more officially if that's all right with you." He pointed to Lilly's folded up list of demands that was lying on a table. "Then you'll have to meet Congress. I'll call for an emergency joint session in a couple of hours. Right now I have to go and pay my condolences to the first family…or former first family. When things settle down in a few days, we will hold a memorial service and honor the president for the good man he was."

There were no words for the joy that Lilly felt. Her dream of vampires and humans living together in harmony was taking a giant step forward. She felt guilty that Ryan's dad only had this new power due to a horrific accident, but she couldn't let her mind focus on that.

"We should start evacuations," Ryan suggested as he looked out the window. "We should minimize the population of D.C. as much as we can. We've seen the havoc Koyt can cause."

"Also, if you could call Dr. Crews and let him know we are ready for his weapons, that would be great," Lilly added.

"I'm glad you're on our side. You seem to be thinking two steps ahead of everyone else," the president noted.

"He was going to load a semi, but that would take time for me to get another vampire to him. If you could send a few choppers it will speed things up."

"You don't happen to have his number on hand?" the president asked, but it looked like he had already guessed the answer.

After entering in the number Lilly gave him, he talked briefly to Lex's father, then sent one of his secret service detail to arrange the helicopters.

"Ryan, why don't you find some place this young lady can lie low for the next two hours."

"Already on it, Dad." He winked.

The presidential living quarters were spacious to say the least. There were several bedrooms; a massive kitchen and dining hall; a treaty room, in which Lilly wondered briefly if that's where they would sign her demands; several sitting areas; an oval room; and more. It was amazing how quickly the other family had been moved from the presidential residence. They really didn't give them any time to mourn.

Ryan resided in the west bedroom. Since the east bedroom was empty and just across the hallway from her friend, Ryan offered it to her.

The room was much larger than hers at home. There was a fancy crystal chandelier in the entryway. Her bed was large with four posts and a canopy over it. The comforter was the brightest white she had ever seen. There were two antique nightstands on either side of the bed. To the right was a sitting area with a small sofa and two upholstered chairs with little foot stools. Behind the sofa were two tall bookshelves, loaded with reading material.

The room smelled wonderful too. There were several vases filled with flowers spread out through the room.

"Can I get you anything?" Ryan asked.

Lilly laughed. "I think I'll be fine."

"Okay," he said, pointing to the door across the hallway. "I'll be there if you need anything. If not, I'll come get you when the emergency meeting with Congress is in session."

"Thanks, Ryan. I appreciate all you've done for me. Lex is getting the treatment she needs."

"I'm just glad this will all be over soon. Then we can finally find out what normalcy feels like."

"Wouldn't that be nice."

Lilly watched Ryan enter his room before shutting her door. It still pained her to look at his stump and remember that it was her fault he had lost an arm. If she hadn't begged him for medicine to save her parents and the rest of her community, then he would still be whole.

Even though Ryan would be furious with her, he needed to be evacuated too. Lilly would add that request to her list of demands if she thought it was necessary, although she didn't think it would take much persuasion to convince the president to send his son away.

Chapter XIV

SPECIAL HEARING

The books in the sitting area were calling Lilly's name. It had been ages since she had the time to just relax and curl up with an exciting read. It still felt a little wrong, what with everything going on, but since waiting seemed to be the order of the day, she decided to indulge.

She ran her finger along the spines, reading each title. Some of the covers were torn and hard to read. Finally Lilly paused over a worn hardback that jumped out at her, *The Count of Monte Cristo*. It was a rather thick book, but Lilly had always been fascinated with royalty and the European aristocracy.

After nestling into a chair, Lilly opened the book and became lost in the story of Edmond Dantès. He had just broken out of prison when a knock on her door pulled her from the tale.

She glanced at the page number to be sure that her place was marked and dropped the book onto the chair she'd been reading in.

Ryan stood there, dressed in a dark blue pinstriped suit. His hair had been gelled and he had shaved since their last meeting.

"It's time."

Her t-shirt and jeans made her feel seriously underdressed. She glanced down, feeling slightly uncomfortable.

"Don't worry, you look amazing." He glanced up and down at her and then offered her his arm.

She linked arms with him, shaking her head. "Lying isn't becoming of a gentleman."

"You obviously have never looked at yourself in a mirror."

"You're crazy." She laughed, bumping him teasingly with her hip. Although, she knew Ryan believed it. Tread was certain that her friend was in love with her. But nothing would ever come of it, so it didn't matter to Lilly. Ryan was a good friend and if he did have those feelings, she just hoped he would never try to act on them. "So where is this meeting taking place?"

"In the press briefing room." He took a turn, leading her down a hallway.

Seeing Congress was a bit of a letdown and a relief all at once. Lilly had never paid much attention to politics. But in old movies it was much larger. Now there were fewer than a hundred senators and legislators sitting in the folding chairs.

"I don't see your father," Lilly whispered as they stepped inside.

He laughed. "The president will be the last to arrive. He doesn't do waiting."

Lilly and Ryan took seats at the front of the room. The rumor of a vampire being in the White House had definitely made the rounds. Wide, scared eyes stared back at her when they did make contact. For the most part, they averted their eyes from her direction.

Ryan reached out and took her hand in his as a symbol of solidarity.

A few minutes later, President Silver walked in, followed by his security detail. Everyone began to stand at his entrance. He went straight to the microphone and waved everyone back to their seats.

"We are at a critical point in our nation's history," he began. "Unbeknownst to all of you, along with the general public, we have been threatened. All of you have seen the horrific attacks on Kansas City and St. Louis on the news. What you don't know is that this is the work of a vampire called Koyt, a vampire that even many of his own species fear. Koyt has given me an ultimatum. I am to turn over control of the United States to him or he has promised D.C. will be his next target."

There were gasps throughout the room; a few of the women began crying.

"As you have all seen, this army of vampires is virtually unstoppable." He paused, Lilly assumed to let his words sink in.

"We have another option. It is our only hope if we want to survive this. What I am proposing may sound insane, but I ask that you keep an open mind. It is our only chance at survival…We must make a truce with the vampires who oppose Koyt."

"No!" several members of Congress called out.

"They'll just kill us!"

"They're monsters!"

The president held up his hand for silence. "I understand your concerns. I've had them myself, but I want you to listen."

He motioned Ryan forward.

"As many of you know, my son was kidnapped over five years ago. What many of you don't know—a truth he hid from the public and me until recently—is that he was saved by a vampire. The reason for his deception I think is obvious: he thought no one would believe him. But now, at this moment, I urge you to listen to his story."

President Silver stepped back, allowing his son to approach the microphone.

"Um, thank you for coming. I want to apologize for not being forthcoming with the facts until now. I was abducted a little over five years ago. I was enslaved in a community run by a sadistic vampire, referred to as Lord Steel, who used his slaves as human blood bags." He turned and pointed to Lilly. "Lilly, a sunwalker, came into the community. She befriended many of the humans and ultimately killed the leader. She has always hoped to live side by side with humans."

There was a loud mumbling as Congress started whispering to each other. It was hard for Lilly to make anything out with so many people conversing at once, but they all seemed to be in shock.

"Lilly offered the humans the option to leave or stay and for both species to try to coexist. I chose to come home, but have stayed in contact with her. Her community has many humans living and working side by side with vampires. A council made up of representation from both species runs their city.

"My father has seen this with his own eyes," Ryan added before returning to his seat.

The president returned to the microphone. "I have seen the city and witnessed the ease at which the humans and vampires work together. The trust between them is something I would not have believed had I not seen it with my own eyes.

"Lilly and her friends have volunteered to come to our aid. Her numbers are smaller, I won't sugarcoat it. However, we believe between her group, the VAS, and some new technology that we stand a fighting chance.

"Things need to change. If they are to fight side by side with humans, risking their lives, we can't go back to how things currently are after the fight. Lilly and I have had some discussions and have come up with some changes we believe are reasonable."

"What sort of changes?" a man in the front row asked.

"Well to start, every vampire would register with the United States."

Ryan's dad was smooth. He started out with the least offensive request. One that might actually give the humans comfort.

"We would build vampire prisons," the president continued. "They would have equal rights and be treated as such."

"That's insane. They'll just kill us all as soon as they enter our cities," a woman a few rows back called out.

"We can't ask them to fight for us and give them nothing," he said tiredly.

"I want to hear from the vampire," another person shouted.

It was silent for a moment. The president invited Lilly to the podium.

"How do we know you won't kill us?" a man in the back asked.

"There is nothing I can say that will reassure you a hundred percent. Only time and trust can convince you of that. What I can tell you is that not one human has been harmed by a vampire in our community. There are good vampires and bad vampires, just like humans. I was born this way. I lived in a human city for most of my life. I went to school and had human friends. Until the government posted my picture up stating that I was a vampire, no one knew. I blended in because I have the same feelings and desires as you do. We all just want to live in peace and find a little joy in life. I have human family and friends. I've never killed a human. I don't feed on humans. Vampires can survive on blood bags. I have even talked with a doctor who is close to developing a synthetic blood."

She looked over the crowd. "I won't lie to you. Or hide things from

you. We survive in our city because the humans voluntarily donate blood. I hope this won't always have to happen. We're not monsters. But we have to eat to survive. This has been the best idea we have come up with."

"How many vampires are there in the United States?" a woman sitting on the far right of the room asked.

"I don't know. I meet new vampires from time to time and haven't traveled extensively."

"Then how can you speak for them?" she continued.

"I don't speak for every vampire. All I know is that most of the vampires I have met are kind and decent. I am sure there will be some that oppose this new lifestyle. Just like there are humans who steal and kill and fight against the government. That's why we need to build prisons. Vampires will have to follow the same laws; if not, they will be hunted down and put on trial."

Ryan's dad motioned to someone in the back who turned the lights off. A screen lowered down from the ceiling. Images of the two cities Koyt had destroyed played on the screen.

After Lilly returned to her seat, the president stepped back up to the microphone. "I am already evacuating the civilian population. It's up to you to decide to ratify this new amendment allowing us to coexist. But the time is ticking by. I've known most of you for several years. You know I am a pragmatist. This is it. It's a gamble, but based on what I've seen, it's the best one we have. I leave this in your hands."

As the president moved to the door to leave, Ryan motioned for Lilly to follow.

The video was brilliant. Lilly noticed Ryan's dad left it playing when they exited, a constant reminder of what lay in store for D.C. if they didn't band together.

"They could be in there for a while. The Senate and House rarely agree on anything. They'll vote together to save time. But still there is no way to guess how long it will take until they come to a decision." President Silver rubbed his right eye.

There were shadows forming under his eyes and he had a five o'clock shadow. His tie was slightly crooked and the back of his suit was wrinkled from sitting for long periods of time.

Lilly knew the feeling. She was exhausted much of the time, as she assisted in running Spero. The entire United States of America must take up a tremendous amount of time. She wondered if Ryan's dad ever slept.

They went back to the president's quarters and Ryan made himself and his father a ham and cheese sandwich. Before his dad had even taken a bite, he was called away to another meeting.

"I guess I'll take this to-go. Thanks son." He patted Ryan on the back as he headed out.

After Ryan finished his sandwich, he pulled out a deck of cards and taught Lilly a new game. It was called Skitty Skat. He dealt three cards and the first one to get the closest to or obtain thirty-one points in one suit won. It was an easy game and it helped to pass the time. There didn't seem to be a lot of strategy involved. It was more a game of luck.

Lilly had never really played card games before. They had been more of a board game family growing up.

After they had played multiple hands, Ryan taught her a game called Fifty-Two Pick-Up. He seemed to think it was funny before they played. Lilly had gathered all the cards back together before they hit the floor and when she threw them in the air for Ryan's turn, his mood wasn't as jovial. The point of the game escaped Lilly, and it took Ryan a lot longer to pick them all up.

He declined to play for a second time.

A VAS agent came in and handed Ryan a sealed envelope.

"It's from your father," the agent explained. "He's caught up in evacuation plans."

Slowly, Ryan used a butter knife to rip open the top of the envelope, careful not to tear the letter. He unfolded the paper and read it silently.

"You did it." He beamed. "Congress has agreed to all the terms and all my father has to do now is sign it into law. Which he says he will do tonight with you."

"Your father sure is busy."

Ryan pushed a strand of hair behind his ear. "Evacuating an entire city isn't simple. Roads are still unsafe. Hopefully that will change soon. It is taking him a while to round up the few commercial planes that are still in service. It will take nonstop flights until Koyt's deadline to evacuate everyone."

"It's a tight schedule all around."

The next couple of days were torture. Lilly had no idea what was going on back at home, Tread still hadn't come back from Colorado, and all she could do was sit in her room and read.

Ryan had been evacuated. After the president came with the official paperwork making all vampires who registered with the United States equal citizens, Lilly made one final addendum.

At the moment Ryan hated her, but he was safe in the facility where Lex was getting treated. They had each other for company. He had forgiven her for worse things, so Lilly had hopes he would get past this too. Plus, he had left his phone outside her bedroom door before he left. So she was taking that as a good sign.

Jane Eyre, The Count of Monte Cristo, The Merry Adventures of Robin Hood, The Hobbit, and *King Arthur and His Knights of the Round Table* adorned her floor. She had finished all of them and wasn't sure if she wanted to start another one. Not because she hadn't enjoyed the others, but because she felt so useless that it somehow felt better to sit and sulk.

The supplies from Dr. Crews were supposed to arrive today, as well as Alex and the other vampires. Then she would finally feel relevant. The president had assigned her over security for the White House. Today she would arm their tiny army and set up their defenses.

At first Lilly felt excited at the new position, but now as she laid a blueprint of the White House and its perimeter out on a table, it felt daunting.

The watch tower positions stationed around the perimeter would be one of the more dangerous posts. Who was she to play God and choose who took those? The other most dangerous post would be guarding the president. Lilly tried to convince him to leave with Ryan, but he refused, telling her "a captain always goes down with his ship." He assented to staying in a safe room. Lilly would be stationed there. That was her easiest decision. Koyt would come for the president. So her position would carry the most danger.

She began penciling in names at various points on the map, only to erase them. Over the past couple of weeks, many of the vampires from Little Rock had become her friends. How could she sentence them to death? The positions on the roof seemed the safest, if you could call any place safe. But how could she place her friends there only to sentence the vampires she hadn't gotten to know well on the wall? Their only crime was that they hadn't had the chance to meet her.

Frustrated, she pushed the papers off the table and dropped the pencil. There was no way she could do this. Guilt was eating away at her already, just because they had volunteered to fight a tyrant. One she and Tread should have dispensed with months ago.

Volunteers. That was the only fair way to assign the posts. She'd wait until Alex and her team arrived and see where they'd like to be positioned. If something bad befell them, it was still on her, but at least they would have had a choice.

There was heavy breathing coming from the hallway. Lilly opened her door and a young man jumped back. He was dressed in a VAS uniform and was trembling slightly.

"You're needed at the front gate," he began, his voice shaky and uneven. "There is a group of vampires waiting there. The president wants you to verify that they are with you."

If they weren't with me, they'd already be through the gate and have murdered half of you guys, Lilly thought to herself.

The night was quiet and clear. No wind was blowing, and the only sound she could hear was the rapid heartbeat and heavy breathing of her escort.

There was a long ladder that led up to the guard tower.

"After you."

It only took two giant leaps before she reached the top. The guards jumped as she landed.

In hindsight it wasn't the best move. One of them drew their gun.

"No," the other one said. "This is her. The vampire that has been staying here."

Slowly his coworker lowered his weapon.

"Sorry," Lilly apologized. "I didn't mean to startle you."

A big eighteen-wheeler was parked alongside the front gate. It was heavily dented in the front. Lilly assumed they didn't stop to remove road debris and just drove straight through.

Bear was sitting on the top of the eighteen-wheeler next to Kenneth. They both waved at the sight of her. There was a group of them talking behind the big rig, so Lilly couldn't see them all. She assumed Alex was there.

"Let 'em in. These are my friends."

Lilly turned to jump back down and greet her friends as she saw her little escort was finally making it to the top.

"We're done here. Time to go down." She offered him a small, apologetic smile. Then she placed one hand on the railing of the guard post and pushed herself up and over the side.

"Wow!" a guard exclaimed when she landed.

The vampires began filing through the gate, many carrying big duffle bags filled with the items they raided from the VAS facilities in Arkansas. Lilly greeted the ones she had more of a relationship with. Even with all the VAS positioned on the walls, none of them seemed remotely close to being as nervous as the humans.

She turned to her human escort. "Can you show them to the Treaty Room?"

His face went pale, as if her suggestion shocked him, but he nodded.

"I never got your name?" she asked.

"It's Stanley, ma'am."

She had never been called ma'am in her life. It made her feel so old, even though the man in front of her had to have at least a couple years on her.

"Stanley will show you to our meeting roooooooom," Lilly squealed the last part as strong arms hoisted her off her feet and spun her around in a circle.

When she was finally set down, she turned to see Tread standing before her.

"Tread!" she jumped into his arms and kissed him. The kiss however was ended quickly, as the vampires all began making catcalls. Embarrassed, Lilly pulled away.

"What are you doing here? Where's Alex? Where's my mom? Was Jimmy telling the truth?"

"Whoa, slow down. I'll explain everything. Let's get inside."

As they followed behind the train of vampires, Tread began to unfold his story.

"Jimmy was being truthful. He led me to a house where I got eyes on your mother."

"Is she okay?"

"I think given the circumstances, she seemed to be faring far better than we expected. But Jimmy was right. Koyt left the house well protected and heavily armed. They had plenty of VAS dart guns. Who knows what else?

"I'm sorry, Lilly. Maybe it's selfish of me to have come here. But I couldn't bear the thought of you fighting Koyt on your own," he said apologetically.

"So you just left her?" Lilly asked.

"Of course not. There was no way for me to get her out. Our only chance was to wait for tomorrow night when Koyt attacks. His goons will be leaving in the morning. They have a vehicle similar to Vanessa's. When that happens there will only be a few guards. So I sent Alex. She left with Van and Jimmy. I armed them with some of the tech you left. Alex will bring your mother home."

Lilly hoped he was right. She couldn't imagine surviving tomorrow night only to lose her mother. How could she ever face Dylan and Adam?

"Lilly, something occurred to me on the way here," Tread whispered. "We need blood and lots of it. Everyone needs to fuel up and we need blood on hand after this fight to heal us."

"I don't think we can ask all of these people to donate blood. It's too soon. They need to see that we are on their side first. We need to earn a shred of trust first."

He laughed. "No, I was thinking of raiding the hospital here. They're evacuating the city, so the humans won't have need of it."

"Oh, that's a good idea." She smiled, sliding her hand into his.

He scoffed. "You say that like it's surprising. When are my ideas not superb?"

"Just wait until after the briefing. I need help making the assignments for tomorrow night. Figuring out where everyone should be stationed."

Stanley led the group to the Treaty Room and then took a seat in the furthest corner.

It was a tight fit, but Lilly wasn't sure what other rooms were not occupied. And this area seemed to have the smallest number of humans for them to scare.

"I just need to grab some papers from my room." She dashed off and was back a few seconds later, with big sheets of paper rolled up under her arm.

"First, I just want to thank all of you for coming. I know you are risking your lives to be here."

She dropped the papers on the big table and began to unroll them.

"The president has agreed to our terms. He signed a new amendment that goes into effect the morning after Koyt's deadline. We will have equal rights and will no longer be hunted by the VAS as long as we follow the laws of the land.

"About the only thing we know for sure is that Koyt can't strike until nightfall. He didn't create an army only to not use it. These," she began, pointing to little red Xs she had drawn on the map, "are where we want vampires to take up positions."

The vampires began to huddle around her, looking at the map.

"Obviously the spots on the wall will be the most dangerous because that will be the first line of defense. Do we have any volunteers?"

"Where will you be?" Rob, one of the vampires skilled enough to have earned a dragon steel weapon asked.

"We all know Koyt is the most dangerous. There is no way of knowing which way he will attack. In the chaos of five hundred-ish vampires ambushing the White House, it will be easy for him to blend in. What we do know is that he will go for the president. So that is where Tread and I will be positioned." She placed her finger on the map to indicate where the president would be.

"I'll take the front gate, dead and center," Bear announced.

As Lilly began to pencil in his name, others slowly began to call out positions until all of them were taken.

"There will also be VAS officers on the watch towers and scattered throughout the ground. One hundred in total."

"These aren't very good odds, are they?" Rob asked, not really expecting an answer.

"We have a few tricks up our sleeves." Lilly winked. "If you all are content with your positions, it's time to weapon up."

A few vampires began to unzip the black duffels.

"No, let's bring those with us. We are meeting the VAS officers in the Press Briefing Room. We have a few more toys to show you."

Tread raised an eyebrow curiously. He knew she had gone to Dr. Crews, but there had been no chance to explain what she had found.

"Did you get your suit?" she asked, looking him over.

"Yep." He smiled. "I've got it in my bag with our axes."

"Why aren't you wearing it now?" she scolded him. "Just because Koyt promised not to attack until tomorrow doesn't mean he will keep his word."

"You have yours on now?" he asked, staring her over.

"Of course."

She was wearing a long-sleeve charcoal gray shirt and black cargos. She lifted the edge of her sleeve up to reveal her suit underneath.

"Okay." He sighed. "I will put it on when I get back. Save me some good tech." He winked. "I really should get the blood and come back. I'll take Eloise and Timothy with me."

"Be careful and hurry back," Lilly pleaded.

She wondered if he had specifically chosen his companions on the fact that they each had a dragon steel weapon, or if that had just been a coincidence.

It was hard for her to let go of his hand when she had just gotten him back. He pushed his way through the crowd, whispering something to Eloise and Timothy as he passed them. Lilly turned back and led the others to the Press Room.

Chapter XV

PREP

The chairs had all been moved out at her behest and long tables had replaced them. Each table held two black crates which were open. The VAS soldiers were already there and stayed to one side of the room, as far from the vampires as possible.

"Stanley and Bear, can you assist me?" Lilly asked.

They quickly came to her side, Stanley seeming a little less nervous than he did before.

"We are going to outfit everyone with weapons for the attack tomorrow," Lilly announced. "I need everyone to come forward and line up."

The humans slowly made their way forward until they were standing side by side with the vampires. There was still a clear invisible barrier, a couple of feet in between them.

"Bear and Stanley," she gestured to the two men, "are going to assist me in making sure you have the appropriate weapons based on your position.

She turned to Stanley and motioned him towards a table. "Stanley, I want you to give everyone a dart gun along with fifty darts."

"Bear, I want you to give all the vampires a pair of earplugs." She pointed to another crate, and he headed over to it.

"These," Lilly held up a small device, "amplify sound. It can be debilitating, at least momentarily. Humans can't hear the frequency. That is why only vampires need the earplugs.

"Our goal is to use these first. If it can halt them for even a few seconds, the darts should help us begin to even the playing field."

After reaching in her pocket and inserting her own earbuds, she pushed the button. A high frequency emitted, toppling over all the vampires, except Lilly.

She waited a minute before shutting it off. A few of her species were able to push through the pain of the sound and stand back up.

She took her earplugs out and placed them back in her pocket.

"After we use these, we will use one again, but we'll play it over the PA system. It will be ten times louder, giving us one more attempt to put down as many of Koyt's army as we can."

"A little warning next time," Rob pleaded.

"If you'd had a chance to be prepared, that would have ruined the point of the exercise. There is one last item that we have in our arsenal." She picked up a small black device. When she turned it on, a blue line appeared. "This is a stun gun. You may be familiar with them. But this one has been tweaked." She winked. "These emit a thousand milliamps. For those of you unfamiliar with these terms, like I was, two hundred milliamps will kill a human. So be very careful with them. These are one of our last lines of defense, to use during hand-to-hand combat. Now I am not going to volunteer to test this out, but it should be enough to stun a vampire for at least a couple of minutes."

"I'll give it a go," Bear volunteered with a shrug.

Her eyes widened, "I don't think we need a preview."

"Sure we do!" Kenneth cheered. Others joined in and began chanting, "Bear! Bear! Bear!"

Lilly noted that even a few of the VAS officers joined in on the chant.

"Fine," she relented, "but don't expect me to do it." She handed the taser to Kenneth who had stepped up, a little too eager to stun his friend. "And don't come crying to me when it's over," Lilly added.

That was one very big difference between men and women. Men with all their testosterone liked to show off and one up each other. Lilly knew plenty of uber competitive women, but she couldn't imagine any of them volunteering to receive a substantial amount of pain, especially when there was no need for it.

Bear stood a few feet in front of Kenneth, looming over him. He puffed up his chest and squared his stance, nodding to his friend that he was ready.

In truth, the mere size of Bear might have shed doubt on some that this small little black device could do him any harm. But Lilly had experienced the pain of electricity, and from what Dr. Crews had told her, it was at a fraction of the level of his creation.

Kenneth turned on the stun gun and a blue current emerged. "Still time to back out."

"Bring it," Bear answered back in his gruff voice.

Kenneth stunned his friend on one of his massive arms. The blast of current was so intense that it shot Bear backwards about fifty feet, creating an unintentional entrance into the press room.

Lilly rushed to her friend's side. Bear lay unmoving, his body smoking slightly.

There were cheers erupting from the room. Lilly could hear comments like, "Awesome!," "Way to go Bear," and "Can I get two of those?"

The massive vampire lay unmoving. After a minute he slowly began to blink and Lilly could see his fingers start twitching. After another minute he slowly sat up.

"That may have been," he said very slowly, rubbing the back of his head, "the stupidest thing I've ever done in my entire existence."

'Um, you think?" Lilly asked, shaking her head.

He stood up and brushed himself off. "I don't even know if I want to carry one of those on me," he added seriously.

They walked back slowly into the room and Bear took a seat on the steps, still trying to recover.

A war was upon them. They would be fighting for their very existence in under twenty-four hours. Some among them believed that it was noble to fight by any means necessary to secure that survival. But Lilly had been close to the edge before. Humanity was a precious gift. It could be squashed easily if not careful.

For that reason, Lilly didn't tell them about the last weapon Dr. Crews had sent over. They were stacked safely away in her room. Six black crates filled with guns.

All of the other weapons Lilly had more or less experienced herself—getting shot by darts, the high frequency sounds. Both were debilitating. And although the new shock weapon had not been used on her, Lilly was very familiar with the pain from electrocution.

These new guns, however, seemed to cross a line. They were torture dispensed in little glass vials. Although never having experienced it herself, Lilly could only imagine how excruciating having your body burn by hydrochloric acid from the inside out could be.

Perhaps if they lost, she might regret her choice. But if war changed her into someone she didn't recognize or couldn't stand to look at in the mirror, wouldn't that be its own kind of loss?

"Was there anything else, Lilly?" Kenneth asked.

Glancing up from the podium, she realized everyone was still standing there, waiting for her to either continue or dismiss them.

After clearing her throat, she said, "That's it. I'd recommend taking some time finding your post and becoming familiar with its surroundings. Meeting those stationed around you might be helpful too." Then she turned back to Bear. "Come on. Let's find you some blood and then you and Kenneth can come back and clean up this mess."

"Yes ma'am," Bear answered.

"I've got it covered," Kenneth offered. "I've never seen Bear like this. Let him rest."

There was still blood in the fridge in her room, so Lilly brought him there. She made him lie on her bed and finish off the last two blood bags.

"Sorry about draining the rest of your stash," Bear noted when he had finished.

Lilly waved her hand. "Don't worry about it. Tread took Eloise and Timothy to raid the hospital. Figured we need lots of blood before and after tomorrow."

"Glad we have some brains running this operation."

His comment stung Lilly at first. She had come up with several good ideas of her own, but then he continued.

"Between you and Tread, I think everything we could possibly do to prepare has been done…" He stopped and leaned to the side, looking around Lilly. "What are those?"

Six large black crates. Lilly didn't even have to look. She knew exactly what had caught his eye. In her haste to get him some blood she had neglected to move them out of his line of sight. Her closet. That was where she had intended to move the weapons.

Lilly sighed. "If I tell you, can you promise to just keep it between us?"

It took him a long moment of silence before he finally agreed.

Lilly explained the weapons, what they did, and her reasoning for not using them.

After listening patiently, Bear asked, "Can I put in my two cents?"

"Sure, why not?"

He walked over to the crates and unlatched the top one and opened the lid.

"Lilly, I'm sure you've thought a lot about this," he began as he ran a finger over the weapons, "and I'll keep my word to you no matter what you decide. But I think you've chosen wrong." He looked at her and his voice softened. "Those vampires out there have come here against incredible odds. They are risking their lives, and the humans are, too. But it's not just about the handful of people here in D.C. You're talking about the whole country.

"Maybe not using the weapons is the right choice for you, but what about all those VAS officers with families? Shouldn't they be given the choice? They have no defense other than the weapons in their hands. There is no possibility for a human to win hand-to-hand combat with a vampire. I don't think it turns you into a monster to defend yourself. They aren't looking to derive pleasure out of how much pain they can inflict. They aren't hunting down these vampires in cold blood. They are simply protecting their homes and fighting for their survival."

"But aren't there some lines that shouldn't be crossed even in a war? Can't anything be justified in the end?" Lilly asked. Everything that had been so clear five minutes ago was now a murky gray.

"Sure, I am certain that even Koyt has his justifications. But I think you are making choices for a lot of people—choices they should be making for themselves. And I'm not sure that someone as kindhearted as you are, Lilly, will be able to handle the losses tomorrow, even if we do pull it off. If they weren't given every option, I feel like you will blame yourself."

Bear seemed to read her like an open book.

"What does Tread think?" he asked.

Lilly shrugged and threw herself on the bed. "I don't know. I haven't had much of a chance to talk to him."

"Like I said, I keep my word." He shut the crate and slid the latch back into place. "I think you should see what Tread thinks. Maybe I'm out in left field all by myself. Whatever your choice in the end, I trust it will be the right one." Bear smiled reassuringly at her before departing her room.

The door to her bedroom opening jostled Lilly out of her dream. The memory of it still left her unsteady. Elaine writhing in pain, turning into a darkwalker, her father's lifeless body in her mother's arms, blood everywhere.

She hadn't intended to fall asleep, and now wished she hadn't. Tread had made it back. He smiled at her as he set his big duffle down.

"How did it go?" Lilly asked, hopping down from the bed.

"Easy peasy." He winked as he knelt down and filled her tiny fridge with blood bags. "Eloise and Timothy are stocking up all the fridges they can find." When he finished, he stood and looked at her curiously, cocking his right eyebrow up. "What happened to the Press Room? It seems a little airier since I left?"

Lilly laughed. "That was all Bear." She told him about the stun gun and how he had volunteered to see how potent it really was.

"That was stupid," Tread noted, shaking his head.

"Bear agreed, after the fact," Lilly smiled.

It was quiet. Lilly wondered how long she had slept for. Tread took her in his arms and kissed her.

"I'm glad you're taking care of yourself and getting some rest," he said and gave her a peck on her forehead.

For a moment she thought of correcting him but decided to let him think what he wanted.

"Wow!" he said, releasing her and turning toward the crates. "When I said save me some gear, I didn't imagine it would be quite that much."

"It's not." She sighed and sat down on the edge of the bed. "Those are the weapons I'm not sure we should use or not."

"Okay." He paused. "Why wouldn't we use them? What are they for?"

Unsure of where to begin, she started with her visit to Dr. Crews and how the idea had made her uncomfortable once time had passed and she had processed it all. Then she told him how Dr. Crews wasn't supposed to send them but did anyway, and finished by telling Tread about her conversation with Bear.

"You're right," he agreed. "It's not an easy decision."

She waited for more. "And?"

"You made a decision and I will support you." He smiled his cocky grin.

"But what do you think? I want to know if you agree with Bear or me. Maybe I'm not making the right decision."

He sat down on the bed and took her hand in his. "Truthfully, I don't know that I am the right person to weigh in on this. I haven't always made the best choices in the past. I've let rage and fear consume me and because of that I carry regrets that will always haunt me."

Since he hadn't really answered the question, Lilly waited, looking at him expectantly.

"I don't know if my opinion is the right one," he said softly. "I guess if I have to pick, I'd lean toward Bear's side. We're the underdogs in this fight. Koyt has us beat on every level. He greatly outnumbers us, he has continued to outsmart us, and he is older than dirt. I think we have to take any advantages where we can. He's not going to fight fair. If it were just us or him, then I'd try to be more honorable. But hundreds of thousands of people will die if we don't stop him."

He took her hand tenderly in his and caressed it. "But like I said, I have plenty of regrets, so I'll leave this decision in your capable hands."

"I think you may be right," Lilly relented. "I already felt myself wavering after Bear's speech and yours just pushed me over the edge." She shoved him playfully.

"Go pass them around," she ordered in a mock tone.

He jumped up and picked up three of the cases as easily as if they were three pillows.

"Wait! First get your suit on. I want to make sure you are protected," she ordered him in a more serious tone.

He laughed. "Yes ma'am."

After setting the crates back down he opened his duffle. He took out the two dragon steel axes and then moved around a few things until the suit was visible.

"There are some cargos and a t-shirt in there for you too," Lilly informed him.

"Cargos?" he asked skeptically. "I've never liked all the pockets. They just seem a little redundant."

"Well you'll appreciate them tomorrow. You have darts, those sound devices, a stun gun, your axe, and a couple of dart guns. I think you need all the pockets you can get."

He shook his head. "I guess I'll give them a go."

It only took a minute to change into his suit and then disguise it under the t-shirt and pants.

He returned walking awkwardly. "I think I'd prefer the suit in two pieces. It's a little snug."

"Don't worry, the material is incredible. It will adjust in a few minutes."

Lilly walked over to a door in her room and stepped out onto the balcony. In the distance, planes and helicopters could be heard ushering the remaining citizens out of D.C. Vampires began to empty the lawns as they sensed the oncoming of the sun.

"Everything changes tonight," Lilly said as she rested her hand against the railing.

A snowflake landed on her hand and she glanced up to see the first snowfall of the season begin to float down from the sky.

"At least there's some peace in knowing that it will be over one way or another in just a handful of hours," Tread agreed, as he slid behind her and wrapped his arms around her. "I love you, Lilly. You've made me happier than I ever thought possible."

She leaned her head back and kissed him softly. "I love you, too. Thank you for opening my eyes to the other half of this world. I can't imagine how shallow my life would have felt without you and this whole piece of me I didn't even really know existed."

The next few hours seemed to pass by like minutes. Tread and Bear passed out all of the weapons and ammo that had been stashed in her room. Tread and Lilly had checked and triple-checked the perimeter with the top VAS agents.

Hours before sunset, she secured the president in an underground bunker with a few of his staff that hadn't been evacuated.

All the vampires had converged together for one last meal. Stanley sat in the corner awkwardly. Seeing so much blood guzzled down by so many was sure to be unnerving, but he hid it well.

An hour before sunset the VAS took their positions. The vampires spread out throughout the White House exits, staying in the shadows, ready to sprint to their positions as soon as the sun slipped behind the horizon.

Armed with walkie talkies, Lilly and Tread headed down to the basement level to guard the Presidential Bunker. Lilly had tried to persuade Tread to stay at the bunker and let her stand guard at one of the White House entrances—just for a few moments until she knew the attack had started, but he had adamantly refused. He would be where she was, end of question.

As they waited, the butterflies in her stomach swarmed around more erratically than she had ever experienced in her life. TV screens and monitors had been installed in the basement for them. Security feeds fed to the multiple TVs. But they could only see what was happening once the main perimeter wall was breached.

"Oh my gosh!" Kenneth yelled into the walkie talkie. "His army is massive. There have got to be a thousand vampires coming toward us." Then he added quietly, "We are all going to die."

Chapter XVI

Lilly couldn't take her eyes off the monitors. It looked so peaceful and beautiful. A blanket of fresh, white snow covered the grounds but any minute now, chaos was going to erupt.

Vampires started activating the sound devices one by one. "They aren't being affected by them!" Bear called over the walkie.

Lilly pushed the button on hers. "Activate the PA System," she ordered.

Normal earplugs could disrupt the frequency enough to just make it painfully annoying rather than debilitating. However, the earplugs Dr. Crews sent were slightly more high tech and would be able to protect her team of vampires from the increased decibels.

A screeching sound rang through the PA system. Lilly could still hear it, but the tones were muted and didn't bother her.

"It's working," Rob called on the walkie. "Open fire."

The guards stationed in the towers began firing their dart guns. These darts should knock a vampire unconscious for several hours.

"There's too many of them!" yelled another voice that Lilly didn't recognize.

Vampires started scaling the wall. The electricity only deterred them for a moment. But the sheer onslaught of numbers overpowered the wall and it began to collapse at the weight of the army.

The human soldiers on the lawns and roof started to fire darts. Vampires began to fall but not at a fast-enough rate. Some of Koyt's army started to reach the human VAS officers. A few humans were able to stun their attackers. But it only took moments for their enemies to realize what was happening and attack the humans at superspeed, giving the soldiers no chance to electrocute the vampire army.

The beautiful white snow began to turn red as the endless army continued to siege the White House.

There was no doubt in Lilly's mind when the acid guns were deployed. Vampires were falling, writhing and screaming in pain, causing many to retreat, but not enough.

Lilly watched, horrified, as two vampires pinned Eloise to the ground and a third decapitated her. Bodies littered the ground near Eloise. *Corpses of the vampires she had killed with her dragon steel?* Lilly wondered. She had put up a good fight, but eventually she had been overpowered.

In the chaos of the fighting, Kenneth had shifted positions. He had been in a tower next to Bear's at the beginning of the battle, but now that many of the towers had been torn down, he was on the ground standing in front of the east wing. There were ten soldiers on the roof above him firing darts as quickly as they could load them.

Kenneth had taken it upon himself to protect them. Lilly had never asked her new vampire acquaintance how old he was. Not that he would have just told her, but by the look of the way he moved, Lilly would guess that he wasn't a spring chicken. Kenneth was swift and precise with his movements. He was holding a long sword, slicing through the oncoming vampires like a hot knife through butter. In his other hand he held a machine gun, firing shot after shot at any vampire who slipped past him.

Lilly wondered if he had been a soldier before he was turned. She was glad he was using the sword so expertly, but worried about Derek. Derek had won the privilege of using that particular dragon steel weapon. She hoped he had just seen Kenneth's skill level and gifted him the weapon as opposed to the other option. Lilly couldn't let her mind go there. She needed to keep a clear head.

A blur of black and blonde soared through the debris and death, coming straight toward the White House. Lilly knew who it was before he paused for the camera.

On the White House's front doorstep, he paused and smiled before ripping the camera off the wall. What sickened Lilly even more was that Phoenix was with him, along with a young boy.

"Get ready," Tread cautioned, backing up so that the bunker was behind him and the only entrance was directly in front of them. In his hand he leveled his acid gun.

Lilly aimed her dart gun towards the end of the hallway. Their axes leaned against the wall behind them.

"Don't hesitate," he warned her. "I'm sure he has some trick up his sleeve."

It was hard to keep her focus; the minutes were ticking by and no one had entered the hallway. The screens literally screamed for her attention. All Lilly wanted to do was look to see who of their friends were still standing, but she held steady, knowing a split second of distraction was all Koyt needed.

Footsteps echoed on the tile. Someone was heading towards them. A moment later, a boy appeared. He was young, perhaps only nine or ten. His hair was blonde and spiky. His clothing was neat and pressed. He wore khaki pants and a blue-collared shirt that matched his eyes, which stared out at them coldly.

"Hello," his voice rang out.

Lilly spared a glance to Tread who seemed equally as stunned. The boy before them was a sunwalker.

Looks like Koyt got his child after all, Lilly thought.

"I've come to offer you traitors a chance to surrender in exchange for a speedy death," the boy continued. He walked toward them without the slightest ounce of fear, his disdain evident in each step.

"Traitors?" Tread choked on the word. "Boy, you have been misinformed. Our only crime is that we cherish life, both human and vampire. This world is big enough for both species."

"Liar!" the boy yelled hysterically. "I've heard all about you. You murder your own kind and put the humans above your own species."

It pained Lilly to see this child who had been twisted and warped by Koyt's perverse version of the world.

"I won't lie to you," Tread began calmly, attempting to pacify the child in front of him. "I have killed other vampires, but only in self-defense."

"I'll never believe you." The boy's eyes were filled with hate. It was difficult to see so much loathing in one so young. Koyt had filled his mind with poison. Yet another casualty of his war. Lilly hoped when Koyt arrived, the kid would be able to see through the psycho's facade for himself.

"Lilly," Tread urged her, "he's a distraction. We need to focus. We'll have to try to convince him later."

Koyt stepped into the hallway with Phoenix.

"Now!" Tread yelled.

Lilly squeezed the trigger and a dart pierced the boy's neck. His eyes seemed to say he was expecting it. There was no surprise as he fell back and hit the floor, his eyes slowly closing, a look of disgust on his face.

It took everything in her not to sprint forward and catch him as he fell. It seemed wrong, although rationally Lilly knew the fall wouldn't hurt the child.

"Cold-blooded, just as I told my friend here." He waved nonchalantly toward Phoenix. His body language was cool and casual but his eyes were fixed on Tread with a look of pure hatred. What did the boy ever do to you?" Koyt motioned to the child on the floor. "He will be my legacy, part of a new generation of vampires that aren't confused about the hierarchy of the world. Never again will my subjects live in the shadows and sewers, hiding from those inferior to them."

"Now!" Tread yelled.

Surprise was their only chance. They both began firing dart after dart. Phoenix dove to the floor as Koyt maneuvered almost effortlessly through the darts. Lilly couldn't believe how fast he moved. Koyt danced gracefully through the passageway towards her as tranquilizer after tranquilizer sailed by, leaving him unscathed.

Before she could change directions with her dart gun, Koyt had knocked it out of her hand. Tread grabbed the double-bladed axe and swung it at his former best friend. Koyt flipped backwards out of the way and pivoted to the right, grabbing the second axe in one swift motion. He lunged forward at lightning speed, plunging it into Tread's side, no longer content with drawing out the battle as he had in the past. Koyt moved aggressively, too fast to give Tread time to react.

The sheer momentum from the blow caused Tread to tumble backward, but he stood up uninjured.

"What the heck?" Koyt asked, looking at the axe as if he'd been tricked. He touched the blade and pulled back his finger, revealing a thin line of blood. The look of confusion on his face made Lilly smile.

Finally, something Koyt wasn't prepared for.

"I'll have to make sure I acquire that secret before you draw your final breath," the psycho noted, a look of awe on his face.

Lilly dived for her dart gun at the same time Phoenix did. It had landed closer to Lilly's aunt, and even with her speed, Lilly wasn't fast enough to beat her.

Koyt, still unsure why his blow hadn't injured his former best friend, instead used his axe to knock Tread's from his grasp and caught it easily with his other hand. Tread took a step back, pivoting lightly on his feet, awaiting his former friend's next move.

Phoenix aimed the gun at her niece. Lilly wondered if she could get to Tread before she was shot and what she could do against an ancient vampire wielding not one, but two dragon steel weapons.

"I have to give you kudos," Koyt admitted. "This is the first time in…well ever, that someone has truly surprised me. You were a lot better prepared than I thought." He hefted the weapons in his hands. "Two dragon steel weapons. This alone would have earned you an applause, but some of the tech you have," he shook his head, "well, you must have better contacts than I do."

"I'm going to kill you," Tread promised, speaking the words slowly.

"You know those words sound a little hollow at the moment. I mean, I have all your toys," he pulled the stun gun out of his pocket. "Took this off of one of the corpses I passed on the way in and after all your other surprises…well let me just tell you, I can't wait to see what this one does."

Tread looked apologetically at Lilly. He felt like he had failed her. Lilly could see it in his eyes.

"You know, it has been a real inner dilemma," he began, sounding almost heartfelt, "deciding which one of you to kill first," he added more flippantly. "But I finally did have to make a choice. I'm going to let you watch me kill Lilly, then, and only then, will I put you out of your miserable existence."

Tread lunged forward but before he could get within striking distance Koyt reached forward with his lightning quick reflexes and stunned him.

Tread flew back into the wall, cracking it and falling lifeless to the floor.

"Huh," Koyt grunted. "Sometimes I don't know my own strength." He shrugged. "I should keep my word. Wait until Tread regains consciousness and then kill you slowly, but I am just so ready to be finished with you." Koyt smiled wickedly before instantly appearing at Lilly's side.

She stepped away from him, her back up against the wall. He grabbed Lilly's throat and began to squeeze it slowly. In vain, she struggled against him. She watched as Phoenix walked over towards Tread and picked up an axe, and horrified, wondered if she'd now have to watch Tread's death.

She struggled, reaching down towards her boot, her fingers brushing against the top of Henry's dagger.

Koyt lifted her off the ground and she could feel her vocal cords being smashed. Pain shot through every inch of her body as it screamed for him to release her.

With her last ounce of energy, she shot her arm down and gripped the edge of the dragon steel blade, barely pulling it up.

It took everything in her to fight through the pain and smile at Koyt.

Koyt paused, releasing his grip slightly. "Come now, what is there left to smile about? I guess I should let you have a few last words. But with you being seconds away from dying, the love of your life about to join you in a moment, and a mother who is a monster and will stop at nothing to kill your father—"

As deeply as possible, Lilly plunged the dagger into Koyt's ribcage.

He released her with a howl as the blade clanged to the floor.

"You fool," he said, hunched over and grasping his side. "Even if by some miracle you beat me, I have still won. Your mother is now a monster, doomed to hunt down and kill your father. I still won," he heckled evilly. "Finish her off," he barked at Phoenix.

She strode forward, the double axe in hand, and raised it above her head.

At the same time, Tread slowly lifted his head. "No!" he screamed.

Koyt smiled gleefully, not able to tear his eyes off of Tread, wanting to watch every moment of misery.

Lilly closed her eyes as her aunt swung the axe.

Tread gasped and Lilly realized she was still alive. She opened her eyes and saw Koyt's head rolling down the hallway, his body in a crumpled mess. A look of satisfaction on the face of her aunt.

"Sorry I couldn't send you word sooner," Phoenix apologized, dropping the axe and letting it clang to the floor.

Lilly threw her arms around her aunt. "Thank you! You saved us," she croaked, her throat throbbing from Koyt's grip.

"Well you stabbing him helped throw him off his guard. Without that, he probably wouldn't have been distracted enough for me to kill him." She hugged her niece back, hesitantly at first and then tighter.

Tread stood up groggily. "Bear volunteered for that?" he asked, kicking the taser far away from himself.

"Bear!" Lilly exclaimed in her hoarse voice, looking at the feeds of the monitors for the first time in ages.

The screens had all gone static.

"We have to help them," Lilly insisted.

"I will. You stay here and guard the president and the boy," Tread instructed.

"I'm coming too. They think I'm on their side," Phoenix said.

Tread nodded and picked up the other axe. "Let's go. We'll be back soon. Lil, I love you."

He scooped up Koyt's head and hurried out towards the ongoing battle.

She nodded, her voice to injured to speak anymore. Once they cleaned up the rest of his goons, Lilly would need to find blood. But for the first time in the last month, she started to hope.

They had defeated Koyt. She was certain Tread could mop up the rest of his villains. And Alex would save her mom. She felt more certain of that now. If they could overcome these odds, stacked so heavily in Koyt's favor, anything was possible.

It was surprising how quickly Tread and Phoenix were able to end the conflict upstairs. Once the mob realized that their leader was dead and that there were two sunwalkers on site, they surrendered.

There were heavy losses on both sides. Tread said many had fled at the sight of their leader's head.

There were a little over seventy-five vampires being surrounded by the twelve vampires who were still alive that had fought on Lilly's side.

Because of the extraordinary amount of bodies that littered the ground, Phoenix, along with what was left of the human VAS squad, was checking them to determine which were dead and which were merely unconscious due to a dart. It was easier to determine if a vampire was dead; all they had to look for was if the body was still

attached to the head.

"I think it's time to let the president out," Tread suggested. "We will have to come to a decision about what to do with the vampires that surrendered."

"I know. It won't be an easy decision," Lilly agreed as she typed in the ten-digit code to the bunker.

The code would turn a light inside the bunker green and then the president, and only the president, could give the order for the bunker to be opened.

Lilly scooped up the still sleeping little boy in her arms. "He has been filled with so much hate. Do you think he'll be able to get past it?" she asked.

Before Tread could answer, the bunker door slowly creaked open.

VAS soldiers peered out, guns pointed through a tiny crack.

"Look, it's Lilly," the president said. "I told you it was safe. She is the only one that knew the code."

He pushed through his squad of protection, making his team uneasy.

"Are they all dead?" the president asked, wiping sweat from his brow with a handkerchief.

"Some surrendered, some fled. But the mastermind behind it is dead, along with countless others," Tread explained. "You'll have some decisions to make. I'd caution you not to be too hasty—yours will set the tone for a new world."

"Very well. Let's give everyone some time to recover. I need to get word out to those on my Cabinet who left, to Congress, and to my son. Let's reconvene in the Oval Office in two hours. We have a lot of work to do."

Chapter XVII

BEAUTIFUL BOY

Eyes slowly began to open, blinking rapidly. The others who had been tranquilized had awoken over an hour ago. Lilly had been worried that he'd wake up when she was in her meeting with the president.

The boy jolted up, and Lilly could see the fear on his face. "Where's Koyt?" he asked as he scooted up against the headboard. His fangs slid down and he growled at them.

"We're not going to hurt you," Lilly reassured him.

"Stay away from me! You killed him, didn't you?" he cried.

"That was self-defense," Tread tried to explain.

"Go get Phoenix. Maybe she can help."

"What did you do to Phoenix?" the child asked as he began to shiver.

Tread left quickly and a moment later the door opened and Lilly's aunt emerged with him.

"Phoenix!" the boy yelled.

She hurried over and swept him up in her arms. "Everything's okay now, Jace."

"They murdered Koyt," he said accusingly.

"Sweet boy, I know Koyt raised you, but he didn't always tell you the truth."

The child pushed her away, looking at her and then at Tread and Lilly. "You're a traitor too. You're just lying like the rest."

"Lilly, can you open the balcony door?" Phoenix asked.

Lilly hurried over and opened it, not sure the need, but eager to do anything that might put Jace at ease. The sun was coming up and Lilly noticed for the first time how red the ground had become. It was striking against the white snow.

"Come with me now Jace," Phoenix instructed. She stuck out her hand and he took it hesitantly.

"Now I want you to walk over to the balcony with Lilly."

"No!" he screamed and ripped his hand away from her. "You'll kill me. Sunlight kills vampires."

Lilly was stunned. This boy was a sunwalker and Koyt had kept him hidden away in the darkness for his entire life, never knowing what he was.

"Koyt lied to you. Sunlight kills normal vampires, but you are special. You can walk in the sun."

"You're a liar," he cried.

Lilly appeared in front of him. "She's telling you the truth. I am a sunwalker, just like you. Do you believe I'm a vampire?"

He nodded.

"If you listen, you can hear my heartbeat," she explained.

Jace paused and listened.

"Now watch." Lilly walked over to the balcony. The sun was rising, and the light was coming closer to the balcony.

The boy's eyes were wide with horror.

Slowly the light engulfed her.

Lilly turned back slowly. "See? It's perfectly fine."

Tread walked over and joined her. "I am a sunwalker too." He stretched his arms out and moved them around in the sunlight.

Phoenix nudged him forward.

The sun hadn't breached the inside of the room, yet each step Jace took was slow and deliberate. When he reached the doorway, he looked back at Phoenix who smiled warmly and waved him forward.

Instead of taking the final step into the sunlight, he reached forward with just his index finger, closed his eyes, and cringed.

After nothing happened, he opened his eyes and marveled at his hand being bathed in sunlight. He stepped forward and let the light engulf him.

"It's really true," he muttered, clearly still amazed.

"It is," Lilly agreed, kneeling down next to him. "I know it could take a long time to trust us, but Koyt lied to you, Jace. Not just about this, but about many things. I come from a city where humans and vampires live side by side. We love each other. We work with each other, we help each other, and we play with each other. My best friend is a human."

"Can I see this place?" he asked skeptically.

"We'd be happy to take you. Maybe in a couple of days. For now, we have to stay here though. I have to talk to the president now. We have to figure out a few things."

His face slumped into a frown. "So I have to stay in this room."

"No, of course not," Tread said, leaning down. "You can go outside, you can explore the house, just stay with another vampire for now. Not all humans are used to us yet. Koyt didn't make it easy for humans to trust us. Stick with Phoenix. I can take you outside later, but I have to go with Lilly soon."

"Jace, where have you been living? Where did you grow up?"

The boy paused for a moment, his brow pensive. "I don't really know." He shrugged. "I've lived in the same place for as long as I can remember. Koyt would visit me, but he always had different vampires watching me." He nodded his head towards Phoenix. "She's the only one I ever liked. But you never stayed long enough," he said accusingly, looking at Lilly's aunt.

"So was it underground, like a vampire community?" Lilly asked, still bewildered by the fact that Jace could have lived so long and been forced to stay in the shadows.

"It was a house. My room was the basement. I only left once…" he shuddered at the memory, "and I never did again. Until Koyt came and got me a few days ago."

"What did you do all day?" Tread asked, still unable to believe that Koyt had kept a child hidden all this time.

"I read. I have three books. Mostly I just sat and waited."

"Didn't the vampires watching you play with you?" Lilly asked.

He shook his head. "I only saw them when they were bringing blood or clothes. I get a new outfit twice a year." He smiled proudly.

It was hard for Lilly not to grab the child and take him in her arms. Fill him with love and human affection he had gone so long without.

"Koyt would come once a year. That's when he'd teach me all about how evil humans are. He would teach me a few fighting moves and bring me my only live meal."

Lilly had to turn her head to keep Jace from seeing the horror on her face. In his whole life, Koyt only bothered to visit him fewer than a dozen times. And during those visits he tried to turn the boy into a monster.

"How old are you?" Tread asked. "Ten?" he guessed.

"I just turned five." Jace grinned, holding his hand up and extending his five fingers.

"You can't be five," Tread argued. "You must have miscounted."

"I know how to count," the boy answered indignantly. "You have a birthday once a year. Every twenty-four months. I've had five."

The monster couldn't even be bothered to visit his prisoner once a year. He made the child think every two years was actually one. How could anyone have lived their entire life isolated and alone? Yet he still seemed rather sane.

"Can Phoenix take me outside now?" Jace asked, seeming bored of all the questions.

"I'm not a sunwalker," Phoenix answered from inside the house. "Only a few vampires have the gift to be able to walk outside in the daytime. But I can take you around the house, and Lilly has a pile of books you can look through."

"Okay, but promise you'll take me outside later?" he asked excitedly, turning back to Tread.

"I promise, just give me a couple of hours." Tread ruffled his hair as he and Lilly headed to their meeting at the Oval Office.

The Oval Office was intimidating. It looked like every movie she had ever seen. It was hard to believe she was really standing there. The president stood and ushered them over to some folding chairs that some of his staff were already sitting at.

"There's much we need to discuss. First, I want to assure you that the United States of America will hold to its promises. I will make a televised announcement shortly. I'd also like to bring a crew back down to your city and video the community. I think it will help ease people's fears." He waved his hand casually. "You know, seeing this already working. Maybe get some testimonials from the humans there. We'll do some promos, get some of them hugging each other, singing Kumbaya, whatever it takes."

The president took a chair at the head of the oval. His chair was slightly fancier It was still a folding chair, but with blue velvet cushions attached to it. It was also bigger than the other chairs.

The seats surrounded a long rectangular table adorned with water bottles and a bowl of cheese puffs. Two blood bags sat in a pottery bowl with ice. It was a nice gesture, but neither her nor Tread would need to eat again for some time. They had both replenished themselves after the fight. Lilly had needed extra. She was grateful Koyt had only attacked her with his bare hands. Her injuries repaired themselves quickly. Had he used one of the dragon steel axes, she would still be recovering.

"The biggest issue is the seventy-five treasonous vampires being held in my Press Room," he began, sounding somewhat annoyed.

Before the sun rose, Tread had all the vampires moved inside.

"Why you didn't just let the dawn finish them off is beyond me," the president continued.

"I don't know that murdering seventy-five vampires who surrendered is the best option," Tread said. "These vampires were probably manipulated and lied to."

President Silver slammed his fist down on the table in front of him. "That doesn't justify the slaughter of my people," he retorted in disgust.

"No, of course not," Tread continued. "But it's not the same for vampires as it is humans. Those who don't interact with humans view them the same way you would cattle. You wouldn't execute someone for killing a bunch of cows."

"That's ridiculous! That's like comparing apples to oranges," President Silver exclaimed in exasperation.

"I think Tread has a point."

Lilly turned to see Ryan entering from behind her.

"Dad, you can't hold them to the same laws that the rest of us are accountable to…not until they are given the same rights," Ryan finished, before taking an empty chair beside his father.

"How did you get here so quickly?" the president asked his son. "I didn't think the chopper had left yet. They told me it would take several hours to fix the damage that was caused during the battle."

"I never left Dad. I couldn't." He turned and stared sternly at Lilly. "I had to fight."

"You were out there?" his father asked incredulously, pointing toward the front of the White House.

Ryan pulled up his right pant leg to reveal a large white bandage around his calf. "It's just a scratch, but I wouldn't be standing here if it weren't for Kenneth. A vampire saved my life. He, along with others of his kind, saved all of our lives. We owe them everything. They deserve equality at the very least."

"How do we know they won't kill again?" an elderly woman wearing large spectacles asked.

"You don't," Lilly answered. "Just like you don't know which humans will become murderers. But once vampires are aware of the laws, then they will be held accountable."

"So these vampires are just supposed to get off scot free? They slaughtered two entire cities—men, women, and children," President Silver reminded them. "What about justice? How can I simply do nothing?"

"What about those anklet monitors I've seen in movies? Do those still exist? Place them in Spero and if they break the monitor off or leave, then they will be hunted down and executed. But first put them on probation," Lilly suggested. "Or assign them manual labor for a time. We'll need prisons around the country to hold vampires. Tread can help with the plans. We've had a little practice with this."

"I'll have to think about this. It seems like a slap on the wrist after the atrocities that have been committed."

"How will we integrate the cities?" A heavy-set man with a thick mustache asked.

"That's a good question, Vern." The president nodded as he reached down and grabbed a bottle of water from the table. After he took a few sips he looked towards Lilly and Tread. "Any thoughts?"

"I think we should start with open registration. Start in Spero, then Little Rock. After two cities show vampires lining up to become citizens, others will follow suit," Lilly responded.

"I concur," Tread agreed.

"I think that's a good idea," Ryan added. "Let's see how many vampires are even open to this idea. At least now they will be given a choice. Then those who don't follow the law with have to answer to it. I believe we will be a lot more effective at rooting out the problem element if we have vampires on our side."

Ryan's phone started ringing. He hastily felt his pockets, trying to remember where he had placed his phone. "Sorry," he apologized quickly. "I think it's for you—it's your number." He flashed the phone to her and Lilly saw her name lit up on the screen.

He stood up and walked over to her, handing her the phone. "Sorry, I need to take this," Lilly said, accepting the phone and hurrying out into the hallway.

Tread followed her out of the room. She could hear Ryan making excuses on her behalf.

"Hello?" Lilly asked, holding her breath.

"Lilly?"

"Alex." Lilly sighed, relieved. "How's my mom? Did you get her? Is she finally back home?"

"Lilly, I'm sorry."

"No! She's dead," Lilly's voice cracked as she choked back a sob.

"No, we found her," Alex added quickly, "but we were too late. She was unconscious and we didn't see the bite mark until later. I'm so sorry, Lilly. Your mom is a darkwalker. I'm bringing her back to Spero. I'll let you decide what to do next."

Words wouldn't form on her tongue. Her feet seemed to collapse from underneath and Lilly fell back. She felt Tread's arms catch her.

He must have taken the phone too because he began talking to Alex. Lilly couldn't focus on the words. Koyt had won. The monster had taunted her during his last moments. Lilly had thought it was a lie. Him just trying to make her doubt, cause her a few extra moments of torment. But Koyt had been honest. Her mother was a monster and there was nothing Lilly could do to change that.

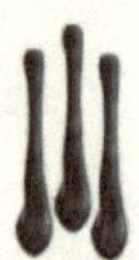

The next morning, Lilly left with Tread and Jace. The boy had been excited to accompany them and to ride on a helicopter. He was curious and seemed very intelligent for someone stuck in a basement his entire life. He had stayed up all night and read as many books as he could get his hands on, peppering Tread with question after question.

She was glad for the distraction. They had suffered losses in the battle with Koyt. There hadn't been time to process it all and she couldn't allow herself to get lost in her grief, at least not yet. Twelve vampires, half of Little Rock's community, had been killed, and Alex still didn't know. Lilly had been so distracted at the news of her mother that everything else had faded away. Bear was the hardest loss for Lilly to handle. They had connected the most in her brief stay in Arkansas.

But fear of losing control made her push even the memories of him away for now. At a later point she would grieve them all and honor them the way they should have been.

There was a small television in the presidential helicopter. They watched the president address the nation. He spoke of the brave soldiers who had ended an uprising against the government of the United States. Brave men, women, and vampires. There was some footage shown, but it had been carefully pieced together to make it look like the victory was easier than it had been.

"See that." Tread pointed to the TV. "That's history in the making." He winked at Jace.

Then the president continued. He spoke about a historical change and a truce with vampires. He announced that vampires would have the opportunity to become citizens. Those who chose not to join and follow the laws of the land would be hunted down. The vampires who chose to become members of society would register. This would start in a new town called Spero where vampires and humans already coexisted peacefully.

Before leaving the White House, Ryan had given Lilly yet another phone. Dr. Crews was going to have Lex call her today. Apparently she wanted to share some good news.

When the phone rang, Lilly was ready to hear something positive.

"Lex?" she asked as she answered.

"I'm coming home today!" Lex exclaimed excitedly.

"Really! You're all healed?"

"All my scans have been clear," her friend replied cheerfully. "I'll still have to be monitored closely. Medicine has come a long way in the last few years, and I was even given some new meds that just got approved by the FDA and haven't even been distributed nationally yet. My dad said after the president's announcement today that it won't be a problem getting most of the equipment to Spero. I'll still need to come back to a bigger city periodically for a few routine tests. But I don't care. I'm coming home today. I'll get to see Ethan and

Luke. I've missed them more than I thought was possible."

"I'm so happy for you." Lilly smiled.

"Did you get your mom back? I heard Koyt was dead but no one could tell me much more than that."

Lilly bit back a sob. "Lex, she's a darkwalker. There's nothing to be done. Either she dies or my father does."

"I've had a lot of free time here, Lil. So I've been thinking about this a lot. What would happen if Koyt really turned your mom into one of those monsters? I had an idea. It's probably dumb, but maybe it could work."

"What?" Lilly asked. "Anything is better than the options I have at the moment."

"What if Dylan were a vampire? He'd technically be dead, right? Maybe if his heart isn't beating, then your mom won't have the desire to drink his blood. I mean, can a vampire feed off of a vampire?"

"Not that I'm aware of. I don't think that's possible. I think you're right though. It does sound like a long shot, but hey, we beat Koyt, right?"

"Wish I could do more," Lex lamented. "I'll see you soon."

The call ended, and for the first time since finding out about Elaine, Lilly felt a spark of hope.

The remainder of the chopper ride was entertaining. Jace peppered them with questions. He loved flying up high and seeing everything so tiny below him.

He was surprisingly well adjusted for someone who had been kept locked up for years. He had vampires feed him and bring him books and visit twice a year. For the most part the poor boy grew up alone, but he didn't seem that different from other children his age.

Phoenix started visiting him the last year. She would bring him toys and play games, but she could only make it over about once a month. Lilly was glad that now he would have a chance to learn what a normal life could be like, surrounded by people on a daily basis.

As Spero came into view, Lilly's stomach became all knots. She wondered what her mother would look like, if Elaine would recognize her.

The walls seemed brighter and shinier. Perhaps sometime soon there would be no need for them. The roof of Town Hall was wide and flat and seemed like the best place to land.

Jace looked nervous.

"What's wrong?" Lilly asked.

"Do you think the people here will like me? Or will I have to go back to my old home?"

She pulled Jace into her arms and hugged him. "I promise, you will never have to go back there. Or any place like it."

The first thing Lilly wanted to do was go find her mother, but Jace didn't need to see that. They hopped down from the chopper and headed straight for the hospital. Tread would meet her at the prison. First, he wanted to let Vanessa know they had returned and he wanted to deliver Koyt's body to her for a burial. He was still her brother, and Tread thought Vanessa deserved that much. Secondly, he wanted to put the gear they brought back into his apartment.

Lilly needed to find someone to watch Jace for a while. Annie or Sam would be a perfect babysitter. Unsure of where Sam was, Annie was the next logical choice. Lilly knew that Annie was typically found in the hospital or clinic.

The hospital smelled of bleach. Adam was a stickler for cleanliness and the smell always lingered on his hands.

Lilly was happy to see both Annie and her uncle were working. Ethan was sitting in a chair, and she realized Luke was on the examining table.

"Is something wrong?" Lilly asked as she stepped inside with her new little friend.

"Can you finish this?" Adam asked Annie.

She nodded and her uncle rushed over and threw his arms around her. "We've all been so worried." He kissed her on the cheek and then took a step back, appraising her up and down. "Well you certainly look in good health." Then turning to the boy, he asked, "And who do we have here?"

"This is Jace. He's a brand new friend."

"Hi Jace, I'm Adam, or some people just call me Doc." He stuck his hand forward and shook the boy's hand.

"What happened to him?" Jace asked, pointing to Luke.

"Don't worry about Luke. He'll be fine. He was climbing a tree and fell and dislocated his shoulder. But in a few weeks, he'll be good as new."

Annie was sliding his arm tenderly into a sling. They must have already reset it. Luke's eyes were red and puffy from crying.

"He won't stay still—drives me crazy," Ethan said shaking his head. "Maybe this will slow him down."

"I need to go check on my mom," Lilly said solemnly. "Do you think I can leave Jace with you guys for a while?"

"Sure," Adam agreed.

"He might be hungry," Lilly added.

"I think I have some cookies hidden somewhere." Adam winked conspiratorially at his new friend.

"Oh, um, that's not the kind of food I was talking about."

Adam shrugged. "Fine, sandwiches and then cookies."

"No, umm, he's on the same diet I am." She smiled sheepishly.

Adam's face went blank. He looked Jace up and down. "Really? Wow, well you've come to the right place. Do you prefer A, B, O negative? We have quite a selection."

Jace looked at Lilly confused. "Don't mind my uncle, he's just trying to be funny. Will you be okay here for a while? That's Annie and she is my good friend. She will take great care of you."

He nodded.

"Okay, I'll be back later. Listen to Annie," she instructed. "Uncle Adam, can you actually come back to my apartment with me? I need to talk with you and Dad. I'll meet you there in a half hour."

"Elaine?"

She nodded then mouthed thank you to Annie in the back and hurried to the prison.

Chapter XVIII

DARKWALKER

Elaine was more akin to a rabid animal than Lilly's mother. But at least they had her locked away in one of the vampire cells in the town jail. For now, she was safe. They had a short amount of time to try to figure things out. Elaine refused to eat, still obsessed over killing Dylan.

Lilly's mother had very little clarity. She was bloodthirsty and frantic, and seemed unable to do anything but mutter a single phrase. So far, the only words she spoke were, "Where is he?"

Looking at her mother through the metal bars was hard. There was no recognition in her mother's eyes when Lilly called out to her. Elaine was filthy, her hair matted and greasy. The clothes she wore were little more than rags. The stench that came from the cell was overwhelming.

A bucket of soapy water had been set inside with a rag, a brush, and a fresh change of clothing.

Unable to stand the sight of her mother, Lilly unbolted the door and turned the electricity to the cell off. When she entered, Elaine continued to mumble the only phrase she seemed able to speak.

"Where is he?"

"Mom, it's me. Lilly," her daughter began.

Hollow, uncaring eyes greeted Lilly. Her mother tried to push past her daughter, still searching for Dylan, but Lilly stopped her.

She struggled against her mother, washing her down as best as she could. It wasn't easy with an unwilling participant. Lilly quickly and forcefully changed her mother into the clean clothes and brushed through her hair.

Elaine was still a mess when her daughter had finished. There was only so much a sponge bath could do. But her mother looked better than she had and the smell was not so repugnant anymore.

The state of her mother left little doubt in Lilly's mind as to how Elaine had been treated. The bucket was a black mess when she had finished.

Lilly held her mother back as she slid out of the cell.

"Where is he?" Elaine continued to ask as Lilly slid the bolt back into place.

"Stand back, Mom," Lilly warned before turning the electrical current back on. It buzzed back into place, shocking Elaine and causing her to jump back from the pain. "Sorry," Lilly whispered, but she knew it was futile. Her mother was not there. At least not on the surface. Perhaps buried somewhere deep inside the vampire that stood before her.

There were only three possible outcomes to this situation. One, they kill Elaine and end this. Two, they allow Elaine to kill Dylan. Neither of those were acceptable to Lilly.

The third was something radical that Lex had come up with. Elaine would be enraged until she killed her husband. But what if Dylan were to become a vampire? He would technically be dead. Would that result in the same rewiring of Elaine's brain that would occur if Dylan died by her hand?

It was a huge risk. What would happen if Dylan changed and then it didn't cure Elaine? He would then have sacrificed his mortality for nothing, becoming a vampire for all eternity. Doomed to spend eternity without the love of his life. Because if option three didn't work, they would have no choice but to end her mother's life.

Her visit to the prison hadn't been a quick one. It was hard to believe this was really happening. That her mother was a vampire. She had needed to see it for herself before she talked to her father and her uncle. However, even having an idea of what to expect, Lilly hadn't been prepared for what she saw.

Lilly opened the door to her family's apartment. Dylan and Uncle Adam were sitting at the kitchen table expectantly.

"Did you find her?" Adam asked, leaning forward.

"We did," Lilly answered. "...but we were too late. She is a darkwalker." Her voice caught on the last word, trembling slightly.

Dylan gasped.

There were several long moments of silence. She gave them time to process the news.

Adam shook his head and sat back down in his chair. "So, what now?" he said, his voice choking back a sob.

"This is new territory to mostly everyone, but we think we may have found a loophole," Lilly explained.

"What do you mean?" her father asked.

Lilly explained Lex's idea to the men.

Adam turned to his brother after a few minutes of silence. "You have to try," he insisted.

"Whoa," Dylan balked. "You want me to change into a vampire? On a hunch?" he asked, stunned.

Lilly leaned forward and placed her hand on her father's shoulder. "It's our only chance."

He hunched over, cradling his head between his hands. "I need a minute."

"Of course he'll do it," Adam said, punching his brother not so lightly in the shoulder.

"There is no coming back from this," Dylan said, his eyes glazed over. "No more daylight...living forever. I love Elaine. Of course I'd do anything to save her. But we don't even know if this will work." He sighed. "Let me see her first. Maybe she just needs to see me. Love can overcome anything, right?" He looked up, hopeful. "Isn't that what all the books say?"

Lilly knew that Elaine seeing Dylan would only make things worse, but she reluctantly agreed. Maybe her father just needed to see it to believe it.

"I'm not sure it's such a great idea," Lilly began, "but if that's what you need to be able to make your decision, then come on."

It was a long, quiet walk to the prison. No one felt like speaking. Even the birds seemed to have gone silent. Every time Lilly glanced at her father, his eyes were looking pointedly at the ground.

Finally Lilly broke the silence.

"I have some more news. Good news I think, but I'm not sure how you both will take it."

The brothers both stopped and looked at her.

"Go ahead, Lil. Just spit it out. Whatever it is."

"I saw Lilly. Your sister…she's not dead."

"What?" they both gasped.

"How would you even recognize her? It has been years…you probably just saw someone who resembled what you think she'd look like now," Adam said, trying to justify Lilly's response.

"She's dead," Dylan agreed.

"No, she's not. She goes by Phoenix now. I know it's her because she looks just like me. She's a vampire. Plus we had conversations about you.

"We didn't talk a lot, but she said your mom died of ALS. She told me she started showing early signs. I know it's very rare at such a young age, but that's what she told me. That's why she chose to become a vampire."

"Why Phoenix?" Adam asked.

Lilly shrugged. "Maybe she just wanted to start fresh. I know she loved you two. I think she's afraid of how you'll react if you see her again…that you won't forgive her."

"Oh Lilly, of course we would," Adam disagreed.

"Do you know where she is now?" Dylan asked, hopeful.

"I think she was planning on going back to Little Rock for a while. At least to meet up with her boyfriend Jimmy. Anyway, I'm sorry to throw this all on you now, but I thought you'd want to know."

Tread and Sam were waiting inside the jail. Lilly gave a brief recap to them of her conversation with Dylan and Adam in regards to Elaine. Both brothers were pretty quiet, still reeling from the fact that their sister was alive.

Tread looked uneasy about provoking Elaine, but led the way down. Adam insisted on coming too.

"Come on, Dylan," Tread said as he paused on the stairwell. "I'll be with you the whole time."

Her father closed his eyes. "Just give me a sec."

Adam pushed past them and headed down the stairs. Lilly followed.

Pacing could be heard coming from the cell.

Adam slowly crept up and peered through the cell. "Elaine?"

She turned and snarled. "Where is he?" she demanded.

For years, Lilly had often wondered if there was more to her mother and uncle's relationship. Even something that they may not have realized. But Elaine's reaction made it clear that at least to her, their friendship was platonic.

Tread came back a few minutes later. "She didn't seem any more frantic to me." Adam shrugged. "She just snarled and mumbled something. "I think it was 'Where is he?' she wasn't super clear.

Lilly turned as she heard footsteps on the stairs. Tread and her father were slowly descending. Dylan tried to put on a brave face, but it was a sad attempt.

"Mom, you have another visitor," Lilly called as they approached.

"Where is he?" she called for a second time, lips curled, revealing her sharp new fangs.

Dylan stepped forward and looked in through the small barred window.

Elaine lunged forward, screaming. Lilly wasn't sure if it was from the electrocution or her desire to attack.

Her father fell over as he attempted to flee from her.

"Give him to me!" she yelled hysterically. "He's mine."

Elaine threw herself over and over at the door.

Lilly half-dragged Dylan back up the stairs, in a hurry to get him out of her mother's sight.

White as sheet was an expression Lilly had heard before, but she had never seen anyone actually lose all their color like that. But now the expression burned into her mind as she looked at her father.

He was paler than she'd ever seen him and he was shaking uncontrollably. "Nooo. Iiit cann't beeee," Dylan stuttered.

Maybe this hadn't been the best idea. Seeing her mother like that must have brought back all the terrible memories of being held captive and having bloodthirsty vampires torturing him.

Lilly waved to Tread to leave. The last thing her father needed in this state was to see him. She didn't know if Tread understood why she was asking him to go, but he complied without hesitation. Sam departed with him.

"Dad, it's okay." She tentatively placed her hand on his shoulder and took it as a good sign that he didn't recoil at the touch. "You're safe."

It took him several minutes to stop shaking. He muttered to himself occasionally, but finally seemed to be coming out of his trance.

"Shee's a mo-monster." Dylan finally said. He took a deep breath and spoke slowly and deliberately. It seemed like he was trying not to stutter. "D-do…you…really…think…we can…fix her?"

"I have to believe it. It's our only chance. Mom will starve in just a few weeks and eventually become comatose. At some point she may not ever be able to be revived."

"So if I…do nothing, she dies." He wasn't asking a question. Lilly could see he was trying to work things out in his head. "If I change into…" he shuddered, "a v-vampire…" He paused a moment, coming to terms with this new situation they found themselves in. "…then there is a chance."

Lilly nodded.

"I don't want to become one," her father explained honestly. "I can't lie to myself."

Lilly's face fell.

"But if I don't, your mother will die. Lilly, I love her so much. Maybe that will be enough to get me through the transformation. I have to try"

The color had not returned to her father's face, but a calmness had set in.

"I'll find Tread." Lilly said.

She returned in a few minutes with Annie and Tread. He had bumped into Annie on his way back to the apartment. It was her turn for a shift at the jail. Lilly had quickly brough Jace to Justin's apartment, feeling it was a more appropriate setting than the prison. Justin was introducing the boy to video games.

"So, when do we start?" Dylan asked.

"Start what?" Tread asked, looking to Lilly.

"Changing me into a vampire," Dylan answered, his voice unsteady and quieter than usual.

Annie put her hands up. "Count me out. I've never tried. I wouldn't even know where to begin. And if you are going to do it here…well then you can just take my shift."

Tread put his hand on Dylan's shoulder. "Maybe you should think this through. Go home and rest. The sun's already setting today and there are some things we need to prepare first. There isn't enough time to get that ready for tonight. We should start the transformation just after sunset tomorrow. Come back here at dusk and we'll proceed from there." He turned to Annie. "I'll take your shift tonight. Will you just make sure Dylan gets home? He's got a lot to think about." Then in a lower voice he whispered, "He might need to talk to someone."

Annie escorted Lilly's father back to his apartment to rest, a look of relief on her face to be getting away from even the discussion of transformation. Once they were gone, Tread turned to Lilly. "I don't think you should stay for the transformation tomorrow. Once it begins the process isn't fun to witness."

"Like that's going to happen," she snorted.

"Lil, I'm serious. Once the transformation starts you should leave. It isn't pleasant to watch, and I can only imagine how much harder it will be since he's your father. Watching someone suffer for hours on end and not being able to do anything about it…why put yourself through that?"

She placed her hand gently on his arm. "Look, I know you are just trying to protect me, but I am not going to let my dad go through this alone."

He rolled his eyes. "I should know better than to argue with you. Your determination can never be derailed."

Lilly grabbed Tread by the arm. "Come on, it's time for a distraction. I can't believe it's already sunset."

"Lex is coming back today. She should get here in a couple of hours." He smiled.

"Yes, and I don't want to miss it. Where is the chopper landing?"

"Alex said Town Hall. I guess if we're going to be frequented by helicopters, we might need some more roofs that are flat and wide." Lilly tugged him by the arm and led him outside. "It was nice of Alex to escort her. After seeing all the news feeds, Lex was a little nervous about traveling without a vampire. Guess I've grown on her. I mean, even though Koyt is dead, it's still hard to know how the rest of the vampire world will react to the treaty."

"Well, let's not give Alex too much credit. I am sure it's purely selfish on her part. I mean, she has gotten used to me being around so much. She probably just misses me." He winked with his signature cocked eyebrow move.

Lilly nudged him in the ribs laughing. "Oh yes, I am sure that's the reason," she said in her most sarcastic tone.

Tread and Lilly raced to the building. Ethan and Luke were already inside waiting. She could tell they were as excited as she was, if not more. Neither one wanted to miss the moment Lex arrived.

"Lex is coming home!" Luke sang, jumping up and down. "Lex is coming home!" Then he stopped quickly and grabbed his arm, pain evident on his face.

Ethan ruffled his hair and shrugged. "Of course he has to dislocate his shoulder the day she comes home. But I'm not even going to worry about that. We've been so excited, haven't we Luke? He barely slept a wink last night."

"Is it time?" Luke asked.

"Almost." Ethan smiled; his eyes began to water. He dabbed at them quickly with the edge of his sleeve.

Lilly put her arm around Ethan and squeezed him lightly. He looked so anxious. "She's okay now. She's going to be fine."

He sighed and ran his hand through his hair, pushing his bangs out of his face. "I think it will be more real to me when I actually see Lex and hold her in my arms again."

They played I spy and a few other games with Luke to pass the time.

Suddenly, Lilly gestured to the roof. "The chopper is approaching. Come on."

Ethan took Luke by the hand and they slowly made their way up onto the roof. The wind whipped around them, and Luke clung to his brother's leg as well as he could manage with one arm.

Tread and Lilly hung back behind them.

As the helicopter blades slowed down to a stop, the side door opened.

Alex, who had been accompanying Lex on the ride back, hopped out first. She reached inside and slowly helped Lex down.

It was hard to believe that her friend was on the mend. She had lost weight and looked frail. Her hair had all fallen out because of the chemo and her skin was pale. But when Lex saw Ethan and Luke, her smile lit up her entire face.

Alex placed her arm around Lex, supporting her, as they met the others halfway across the empty roof.

Luke ran to Lex and gave her a big hug. He didn't want to let go, so Ethan had to bribe him with extra stories before he would release her.

The worry seemed to fall off Ethan as he picked up Luke with one arm and hugged his wife with the other.

"Where did your hair go?" Luke asked as he reached over and rubbed the top of her head.

Lex laughed. "I lost it."

"I will help you find it," Luke proclaimed.

Lex wrapped her arms around her little family.

"Thanks buddy." She said as she kissed him on the cheek and then leaned forward and gave her husband a more grown-up kiss.

Lex turned around to find Lilly waiting. She grabbed her best friendin a hug. "Thanks, Lil. I wouldn't be here if it weren't for you."

Lilly shook her head. "I think it's more because of me that you ended up here."

Lex shoved her in her normal playful attitude, but there was no power behind it. It would take a while before her strength came back.

"You didn't give me cancer," Lex said.

Lilly opened her mouth to say something else, but her friend continued.

"Take me home," she whispered. "I don't want to pass out in front of Luke."

Tread reached forward and scooped her up. "Allow me. We have missed you around here."

"Thanks." She smiled and closed her eyes. "By the way, what happened to Luke's arm?"

"He had an incident with a tree. He'll be fine," Lilly answered.

Tread took Lex home, followed by Ethan and Luke.

Lilly stayed behind. She turned to Alex. "Thank you for riding with her."

Alex looked back at the chopper. The pilot had disembarked along with a nurse and both were standing still, looking nervous.

"It was an odd sensation, walking into a human hospital. VAS watching me but not pointing their weapons at me…" She shrugged. "To be honest, I didn't feel safe until we landed here. It will take time to get used to this new uneasy sense of peace that seems to be beginning."

Lilly walked to the pilot and stuck out her hand. "Thanks for bringing my friend back."

He took it hesitantly. "Are you both really vampires?" he asked uncertainly.

"Yes," Lilly responded. "Why don't you come take a look around, see how we will live, see what peace can look like?"

Alex looked up. "Oh, and I forgot to mention I brought back a surprise. I'll give you a minute." She smiled suspiciously and disappeared inside the chopper.

"Wow!" the nurse exclaimed. "She just vanished."

Lilly turned to see movement inside the chopper and a huge man jumped down from the far side of the chopper. She stared in disbelief. Even before he turned around there was no way to confuse him with someone else.

"Bear!" Lilly exclaimed, running forward.

She leapt into his arms and hugged him.

"You're alive? How?"

He laughed. "Well, you wouldn't think it would be to hard to tell if someone had been decapitated or not, but apparently it was."

"Huh?" Lilly asked, confused.

"I was hit by a few darts during the chaos. Somehow after I fell, a piece of metal debris fell across my neck. When I woke, I was covered in blood. I don't know. I'm guessing it was one of the human VAS officers who checked my body. With the metal and blood, apparently it looked like I was headless." He rubbed his neck. "I'm glad that wasn't the case."

"Me too!" She hugged him again. "Let me take these two around the town, and we'll catch up soon." She kissed him on the cheek and then went back over to the humans.

The pilot and nurse cautiously followed Lilly inside, sticking to each other like glue.

Lilly gave them the grand tour. The visitors seemed to relax as the time passed, especially when they saw other humans interacting with the vampires like it was no big deal.

"Do you think every city will be like this?" the pilot asked after the tour was over.

"I'm not foolhardy enough to believe this will happen overnight. Just look at the past. It wasn't long ago when people of different races were looked down upon and discriminated against. I'm sure there will be ups and downs. Vampires and humans who will fight against this new concept. But we know it is possible." Lilly said, pointing around the city. "It will take time and work, and some give and take on both sides. Someday, yes, I hope this will be the new world norm. I think the president is putting good measures in place that will assure the survival and safety of both species."

Lilly escorted the nurse and pilot back to the chopper, thanking them again for their help. She sat down on the roof after the helicopter left and looked out over Spero. Hope. It wasn't just her fanciful idea anymore, but a real possibility.

To say the last few weeks had been crazy would be a gigantic understatement. They had searched for Koyt and found him, unprepared for him and his nightwalker army. She had fought in a war and won. There were losses, but the end resulted in the government of the United States seeing vampires in a new light. Everything was gray now. Black and white no longer existed.

Koyt was dead. Lilly no longer had to look over her shoulder at every turn, wondering what he was plotting next. Lex's father had turned out to be a big surprise. His invention of synthetic blood could revolutionize the way vampires fed.

He was running his final human tests now. Lex had told Lilly that this was the first batch of synthetic blood that the test subjects were not rejecting. If all went well, vampire testing could begin as soon as volunteers were found.

The last pressing detail was Elaine. All she needed to do was fix her mother. Lilly hoped changing her father into a vampire was the right move. If it didn't work, her dad would have given up so much for nothing.

She wondered if he had really thought through living in darkness for eternity. It seemed so unfair to Lilly that she had this huge blessing that others did not.

"So here you are," Tread said, smiling as he stepped out onto the roof. "What are you doing?"

The sun was shining brightly. Birds were flying overhead, and down below, she could hear vampires and humans working side by side. Life could seem perfect if one just skimmed the surface.

Lilly sighed. "Just thinking…about everything that has happened…that could happen."

He came and sat beside her, wrapping his arm around her. Lilly rested her head on his shoulder. "How long will the transformation take? When can we test it?"

Tread rubbed her arm softly. "It just depends. Everyone is different…a day or two more than likely." He kissed the top of her head. "Why don't you go home and get a few hours of sleep," he suggested.

"I don't think my father wants company right now."

"Go to my apartment. Sleep in my bed."

"I think you're forgetting about Jace," Lilly reminded him.

"I took care of that. He's sleeping at Lex's with Luke."

She wasn't thrilled with that idea. Ethan and Lex deserved their first night back home together to be just with their family.

"Don't worry, it was Lex's idea. She saw him coming out of Sam and Scott's apartment."

Lilly sighed. "Do you think he has been passed around too much? I don't want him to feel like he's a bother."

Tread pulled her toward him and held her.

"No, he's having the time of his life. Literally. I explained to him about your mother and said we'd have plenty of time to spend with him in a couple of days."

"All right. I think I will take you up on the bed." She yawned.

Then Lilly kissed him once, and he pulled her into his arms even closer. After a moment she pulled away. "If I don't stop now, I doubt that I ever will."

He sighed, releasing her reluctantly. "See you soon." He winked.

Lilly opened the apartment door slowly. She could hear the even breathing of her uncle in the other room and didn't want to wake him.

She crept quietly into Tread's room and slid under the covers. She didn't need blankets or sheets to keep her warm, but they were comforting to her nonetheless.

She closed her eyes and breathed in. Now that she wasn't the newbie vampire who knew nothing about her own kind, she could smell the sunshine on the pillow, mixed with a faint hint of bleach.

Living with Adam was definitely rubbing off on Tread quite literally. Her uncle was a neat freak and loved to use bleach.

Lilly closed her eyes and tried to dream of happier times for her family.

Chapter XIX

PAIN

The banging of pots and pans in the kitchen woke Lilly. She rolled out of bed yawning. She stepped out into the main living area and found it empty. The noise was coming from her apartment.

She hurried over across the hallway to see how her father was doing. When she opened the door, Dylan stopped mid-pancake pour.

"Where have you been all day?" he asked, resuming his meal preparations.

"I've been sleeping, but I didn't realize how long I'd slept. I've slept the night and most of the day away."

"Sleeping where?" he asked accusingly, sounding very fatherly.

"At Tread's. Don't worry, he wasn't there." She looked down at his pan, changing the subject. "Pancakes? Isn't it like an hour before sunset?"

"I felt I deserved a last meal." He offered a half-hearted smile. "Human meal at least." He turned red. "That's not what I meant." He chided Lilly after seeing the grin on her face. "I just wanted to savor one more meal of actual solid food, before I change to the all-liquid diet."

Lilly could tell he was trying to take everything in stride, but he looked a little green when he spoke.

Dylan piled up a plate of pancakes and drizzled melted butter on them. Syrup was harder to come by, but they could make their own butter.

Of course that would all be changing now too. Lilly had already sent a group of vampires to start clearing the roadways. Soon, trucks would start delivering supplies to their town. With vampire escorts, the government was going to try reopening the roadways for deliveries. If things worked well, in a few years, normal citizens might be able to start driving across the country like in the olden days.

Dylan cut through the pile with his fork and slowly placed a bite in his mouth. He closed his eyes and smiled.

"Heavenly," he said without opening his eyes.

Lilly watched her father with mixed emotions. She was happy to see him enjoying something so simple, making his last few human minutes matter. However, at the same time, her heart ached that he even had to contemplate giving up his mortality.

She looked up at the clock. "We should go."

Dylan finished the last bite, wiped his face with a napkin, and rose from his chair.

They walked in silence to the prison, each lost in their own thoughts. Tread and Annie were inside waiting.

"I thought I'd run into you earlier in the day," Tread commented. "What have you been doing all day?"

"Stuff," Lilly said vaguely.

"Sleeping," Dylan interjected.

Tread covered his mouth with his hand to keep from laughing.

"Poor Jace. I haven't seen him all day," Lilly said, trying not to look so embarrassed.

"Don't worry, I checked in on him. I was going to see if he wanted to throw the football around. He's having a great time playing with Luke. He barely noticed me." Tread pretended to look hurt. "And how could anyone not notice me?" He flexed his arm muscles.

"Ha. Ha," Lilly said, unamused.

"So, Dylan, are you sure about this?" Tread asked, turning the attention back to the reason they were gathered. "Once we begin, there is no going back."

"Yes, if there's a chance I can save her, I have to try. I couldn't live with myself otherwise. Even if this kills me," Dylan said, trying to put on a brave face. "Lilly mentioned something about me having to drink human blood?" He cringed slightly.

Tread pulled out three blood bags and placed them on the table.

Lilly's and Dylan's eyes widened.

"All that?" her father asked, dumbfounded. "I was imagining more like a shot of blood, or maybe a cup."

"The transformation changes your body chemistry completely. Human blood is what fuels it. I believe the more you have in your system the easier it will be. It's not an exact science."

Dylan nodded but looked uneasy.

"I don't know how much you will be able to keep down, but just do your best." Tread picked up a pair of scissors and snipped the corner off of a bag. He handed it to Dylan.

Lilly's father took the bag hesitantly and then held it to his lips. He sucked in a mouthful and then spit it out, coughing and gagging at the taste.

"We can't do it if he won't drink it," Annie said.

Her father wiped his mouth. "I'll do it," he said firmly. "I didn't know what to expect. Now I do."

He turned to Lilly. "Just talk to me. Tell me anything, I don't care, just try to distract me, so I'm not thinking about what I'm actually doing."

Her mind went blank. Lilly tried to think of something, anything to say, but couldn't come up with a single idea.

"I saw Lex today," Lilly finally said.

Dylan picked up the pouch again and closed his eyes. He slowly sipped the blood. His face was scrunched up and every mouthful was a struggle to swallow. He waved his hand for her to continue.

"She looked good…I guess. I mean, she is alive." Lilly sighed. "Lex was really pale, and her hair had all fallen out. She looked so different, like she's still sick. But I know it will take time before she's her old self again."

After finishing half of the first bag, he paused. He looked like he was trying not to throw up. After a second he opened his eyes. "She'll get better now. Her hair will grow back, and she will get her energy back." He winked. "At least that's what my brother says."

He looked at the blood bag in front of him and took a deep breath before picking it up again. He closed his eyes and drank more blood.

"You really are amazing, Dad." Lilly smiled in awe. "Even when you are doing something more difficult than I think I can really understand, you're still trying to make me feel better."

He finished the first bag, shaking slightly as he did so. "Can I have a few minutes before I try to drink the second one?" He looked to Tread.

Tread shook his head. "Sorry. I think it's better the faster we get it in you. I think the more of the transformation that can take place in the dark, the safer we will be." He looked at Dylan sympathetically. "And we can't begin until you finish." He pushed another pouch toward her father.

Her father nodded, seeming resigned to his fate. Having set his mind to the task, he picked up the second bag and downed it quickly.

Lilly's mouth dropped open in shock.

Dylan's skin looked pale with a light green tinge to it. He closed his eyes and tried to settle his stomach.

"You're doing really well," Tread said as he pushed the final pouch toward Dylan.

Her father took the final pouch. She had hoped he would be able to down it as quickly as he did the second, but almost immediately she realized that was not going to be the case.

It took about ten minutes of Dylan fighting himself for every swallow. But finally he was done.

Lilly could hear his stomach sloshing from all the liquid.

"Okay, let's get this over with before it all comes back up," her father pleaded.

Tread looked at Lilly. "Whenever you're ready."

"Me?" Lilly asked, surprised. "I'm not doing it!" she exclaimed.

"He's your father," Tread argued. "It didn't even occur to me that you wanted me to do it. I just thought I was getting it all ready for you and then I'd stay with him during the transformation. I didn't want you to see that."

"I've never done this before. You have to do it," Lilly insisted. "You changed Red successfully."

"And I failed before that," Tread reminded her.

Dylan shook his head. "You are both instilling so much confidence." He put his hand on Tread's shoulder. "I want you to do it," he said. "Please don't put this on Lilly. She will never forgive herself if something goes wrong."

"And she'll never forgive me if it goes wrong either," Tread countered.

"I think we both know that isn't true. She would be mad for a while but in the end she would forgive you. You both have been through too much to let anything stand in your way."

Tread looked at Lilly. She smiled hopefully. He sighed. "Fine. But I can't make any guarantees. I haven't done this enough to know what works. These are all just my best guesses."

"Fair enough," Dylan agreed.

"Your neck has the best veins," Tread said sheepishly.

"Great." He tilted his neck forward and Tread leaned in. He hesitated for a moment and then locked down with his fangs.

Her father gasped as the vampire forced as much venom as he could into his system.

"It doesn't hurt that bad," Dylan said when Tread finally released him.

"Give it a minute. Your whole body is about to be changed in ways we don't even understand," Tread cautioned. "We should probably put him in a cell downstairs just to keep him out of the way, and out of any sunlight."

Lilly escorted her dad down the stairs and into the first cell. She wanted to put as much space between him and her mother as possible.

For a brief moment there was utter silence as Lilly locked her father in and waited outside. Then, as if a flip were suddenly switched, Dylan was screaming hysterically, begging for them to stop, saying he had changed his mind.

Tread came down the stairs and took Lilly in his arms. She buried her head in his shoulder. "This is horrible," she cried.

"Lilly, go. I will stay with him. You don't need to watch this."

"I won't leave him," she said, pulling away. "I'll be okay. I just, even with your warnings...I wasn't prepared for this."

The hours seemed to drag on. Seconds seemed like days, minutes like weeks, and hours like an eternity.

Lilly felt guilty. More than a few times, Tread's offer for her to leave popped into her mind, and she almost took it. But then she'd remember everything her father was risking for their family and everything he was giving up if this worked, and knew that no matter how much it pained her to stay, she couldn't desert him.

Then a horrific thought occurred to her. What if Dylan didn't survive the transformation? Would her mom still be a darkwalker if she didn't kill him herself? That was the question they were unsure of, but she had never considered the fact that she might end up losing both of her parents.

As the screaming continued, Lilly tried to distract herself. She thought about Lex and how wonderful it must be for her to finally be waking up in her own bed, back with her family.

She was surprised Adam hadn't stopped by to check on his brother. But perhaps Tread had warned him off like he had her. Or maybe he was checking in on Lex and planning to stop by later.

After twelve hours of endless screaming, if you could even call it that, Lilly had to leave. She needed a few minutes. Never in her entire existence had the sound of such suffering pierced her ears. It didn't even sound human. But then again, maybe Dylan wasn't anymore.

The guilt washed over Lilly immediately as she took the steps in a single bound. She glanced to Tread who nodded. Lilly knew he would stay with her father.

Bursting out into the sunlight, Lilly took a deep breath and covered her ears, attempting to lessen the shrieks coming from below.

Being so overcome by the pain of her father, Lilly hadn't noticed Uncle Adam standing off to the side. He was leaning against the building, looking like he hadn't slept in a week. Which he probably hadn't.

"Is it over?" Adam asked, not meeting her eyes.

Was what over? Dylan's transformation? Dylan's life? Elaine being a darkwalker? Uncertain to which of the many outcomes he might be referring to, Lilly simply answered, "No."

"You probably think I'm weak," Adam said, looking ashamed. "He's my brother. My twin. I should be in there with him. I tried. But I can't stomach it. He's braver than me."

"Uncle Adam, I could never think that about you. It's unbearable. I don't blame anyone for not being in there. I even had to come outside and take a break, making Tread have to suffer through it."

He wrapped his arms around Lilly. "I just pray this is over soon."

"And that it works," Lilly added sullenly.

He leaned back and made his niece look into his eyes. "It will work."

"So how are things going with you?" Lilly asked, trying to distract herself. Her uncle may not have been able to hear the screaming coming from inside, but she still could. "Dad said he hasn't seen you a lot the last few weeks. You don't have a secret girlfriend, do you?" Lilly laughed, teasing her uncle.

Red flushed on her uncle's face. He turned away hastily.

"What? I was totally joking. That's really where you've been? Who is it?"

Adam shook his head, turning an even brighter shade of red. "Lilly, just stop. If I was ready to share that, I would have. Don't tell anyone. Besides, I'm thinking of ending things. I just don't think we're compatible."

"Adam, you deserve to be happy. Don't rush into a hasty decision." Lilly said as she racked her brain, trying to think of who it could be. Justin had brought so many new people to Spero, and with her being gone searching for her mom and fighting Koyt, she hadn't had the time to get to know them. "I'm still going to find out who it is." She smiled.

He rolled his eyes. "That might be hard to do because I'm leaving. As soon as I know Dylan and Elaine are okay."

"What—" she began. "Uncle Adam, okay, I promise I won't try to found out who the mystery girl is. Don't you think leaving is just being slightly overdramatic?"

A chuckle slipped through his lips. "Lil, I'm not leaving because of that." He took her hand in his and squeezed it lovingly. "And I won't be gone forever. But you told me Lil—Phoenix, my sister, is still alive. I have to find her. Things will be better here, now that the government is on board. You will be safe."

"There are still vampires outside the walls. Just like in the human world, there may be some who don't want to abide by the new rules. You can't go alone."

He raised an eyebrow. "I can't?" he mused.

"Well, you shouldn't. For a doctor, you aren't very bright sometimes." She shoved him playfully.

"I'll take it under consideration." He turned more serious. "Lilly, will you let me know when it's finished? Dylan's transformation, I mean."

She nodded, then looked back toward the entrance to the jail and the wailing coming from inside.

"I'd better get back in there. Promise you won't leave without saying goodbye?"

"Never." He winked.

Chapter XX

BEGINNINGS

The screaming had ceased coming from Dylan's cell after eighteen long hours. Tread was just coming down the stairs with a fresh blood bag.

"I'll go in first," he offered.

"No," Lilly insisted, taking the bag. "He's my father. I'll go."

She peered through the window and bars into the cell. Tread assured her the transformation went well, but so far Dylan hadn't spoken a word.

In the back of the cell, he sat on a small cot, as still as a statue. Lilly unlocked the room and pulled the solid door open. It squeaked loudly, seemingly jogging her father out of his trance.

"Is..." he began softly at first and then seemed to find his voice, "...is it over? Did it work?"

Lilly started to open her mouth, but he continued.

"I mean, I know it worked. I can see everything, even things far away, my heart isn't beating, and I can hear people laughing and talking outside. It feels so foreign." He looked up at her, slightly terrified. "But the pain…it's finished right?" He shuddered at the memory still fresh in his mind.

Tread stepped in behind her. "Yes, it's over Dylan. Truthfully, I'm surprised it worked, what with your hatred for our kind. But you were right. Your love was strong enough to pull you through."

He sighed, and a smile pulled at the corners of his mouth. "I made it," he said, as if he still didn't quite believe it. "And I don't hate all of your kind. Our kind. It makes it easier somehow becoming a vampire knowing Koyt's dead."

"Here," Lilly said, tossing him the blood.

Quick as lightning, his hand shot forward, catching it and then he immediately sunk his teeth into it.

When he was finished, he looked at them in awe. "That tasted so much better this time."

They all laughed.

He looked at his hands and felt up in his mouth where his fangs had just been. "It's so surreal. I still feel like myself, but at the same time, I don't. I can't believe how fast my reflexes are now. And my canines just extended and retracted on their own, just out of instinct. I didn't even realize how much I needed that blood until I tasted the first glorious drop." He looked at the empty bag. "I'm not going to try to rip out Lex or Adam's throats now, right?"

"Dad!" Lilly exclaimed in exasperation. "When you were hungry and walked by a hamburger joint, did you ever go crazy and start eating someone else's burger? You still have your self-control." She turned back to Tread and gestured toward the stairwell, and he disappeared.

Dylan looked at her expectantly.

"I told Uncle Adam we would tell him if and when you came through it."

"Oh, yeah, that's good."

"So are you ready…" She let the words dangle.

"To see if your mom still wants to murder me?" Dylan shrugged. "Why not, otherwise what was the point to all this?"

He bolted to the door and Lilly grabbed him. "Try to slow down. Let's approach this cautiously."

He nodded, looking slightly embarrassed.

Lilly walked over to Elaine's cell. "Mom!" she called.

A low growl came from inside followed by the phrase that was becoming her mother's mantra. "Where is he?"

Dylan waited for Lilly to move back and he stepped forward, facing Elaine through the small barred window.

Lilly closed her eyes and waited. There was nothing.

Suddenly Elaine gasped and fell backward, screaming hysterically and writhing in pain. Before Lilly could stop him, Dylan unlocked the door and swung the door wide open. He rushed to her mother's side.

"No!" Lilly cried out as she reached for her father but only caught handfuls of air.

Lilly rushed behind him and tossed him across the room positioning herself between her mother and father.

Finally Elaine stopped. Her body lay on the prison cell's floor, completely still. Lilly crept forward and leaned over her mother.

"Lilly?" Elaine asked, confusion masking her face. "What happened? What's going on? I feel like I've been in a heavy fog."

"Mom?" Lilly rushed forward, pulling her mother into a long embrace, relieved to see Elaine had regained her recognition..

"Elaine!" Dylan exclaimed in relief. "You're back."

"What do you mean back?" she asked uncertainly.

"Let's go upstairs and we will explain it all."

Lilly and her father ushered Elaine up the stairs slowly and cautiously as if she were a china doll and any movement could send her shattering into a million pieces.

As they took the steps slowly, Elaine froze.

"Mom, are you okay?" Lilly asked.

Elaine put her fingers on her wrist. "It's real. I wasn't dreaming. I am a vampire."

"Yes," her father confirmed. "Well talk about it more upstairs. You need blood," he said, reminding Lilly that her mother hadn't fed since her transformation, being too fixated on finding and killing Dylan for anything else to have mattered.

Once in the foyer, her father led her mother to a couch while Lilly grabbed another blood bag from a mini fridge they kept behind the desk.

"Here. Drink this. You may need more than one," Lilly said, handing the pouch to her mother.

Elaine hesitantly put it up to her lips and then bit down. She downed it quickly and requested a second bag, which she finished with equal precision.

"It's all coming back to me now; it's like the fog is lifting," Elaine said, closing her eyes. "The whole transition process is kind of hazy. I remember being forced to drink something disgusting, and then I felt a sharp pain on my wrist. I think that's where one of Koyt's goons bit me." She paused, then said, "I can hear Adam now." Her mother looked surprised. "He's coming with Tread." She seemed to relax for the first time.

Adam walked through the door a moment later.

"It's still me," Elaine said hesitantly. "Just different."

"I had no doubt." He hurried forward and gave Elaine a hug and then turned to embrace his brother. "It worked. Finally. We were due a little luck."

They all laughed.

"Yes, it was certainly our turn." Elaine reached for her daughter and squeezed her hand. "Now we'll be a family forever." She turned and reached for Dylan with her other hand. "I always hated the idea of leaving you alone for the eternities. Although this might take some time to get used to." Her mother returned her gaze to Dylan. "I still can't believe that you did this for me." She shook her head in amazement. "After everything vampires did to you."

He leaned forward and kissed her. "I would do anything for you two." He winked at his daughter. "Maybe now you'll really believe it."

Elaine kissed him again. "I love you."

The vampire entrance to the jail opened and Lilly turned to see Annie stepping inside.

"So, it really worked," she said in amazement. "I'm so happy for you Lilly."

Tread wrapped his arm around Lilly. "Me too."

Hovering in the doorway, Annie looked as if she were waiting for something. Tread seemed to have the same thought.

"Did you need something?" he asked.

Annie didn't answer but looked at Adam.

"I'm leaving tonight," Adam explained, turning to his brother. "I'm going to find our sister and bring her home."

"I still can't believe she's been alive all this time. Looks like resurrection seems to run in our family," Dylan commented.

"Oh my gosh!" Lilly exclaimed, looking at Annie and then to Adam.

"What?" Tread asked.

Her uncle's eyes pleaded silently with her.

"Um, nothing. Sorry, I just got the resurrection joke," she lied lamely.

Tread's eyes bore into her, searching for answers, but he didn't press.

"I'll be back as soon as I can." Adam kissed his niece on the cheek. "Take care of everyone."

"You too." She smiled widely.

"What is with you today?" her father asked.

"Just happy."

Her uncle left with Annie, and Lilly tried to stop herself from grinning like a kid on Christmas.

"Let's get out of here. I have spent enough time in this prison." Dylan led Elaine toward the front door and Lilly rushed in front of them.

"What are you doing?" Lilly yelled.

"Going back to our apartment," her father explained, looking at his daughter as if she were crazy. "What's wrong with you?"

"The *sun* is out!" She motioned to a window in frustration. "You have to use the vampire corridors now."

Her parents both laughed. "Oh yeah. That will take some getting used to."

Lilly turned them toward the safe vampire exit, not finding anything funny in the fact that they had just nearly been incinerated.

After watching them walk through the safe exit, she turned to face Tread.

"One of us needs to watch them nonstop!" she exclaimed. "They don't even seem to grasp the significance of what almost transpired."

Tread laughed lightly, and then stopped abruptly as he received a death glare.

"They will get it. Don't worry. So much was piled on them at once. New species, immortality." He cocked his eyebrow up in his signature move and then winked. He reached around her and pulled her closer. "Let's just enjoy the fact that it worked for a moment."

Lilly sighed but complied. She wrapped her arms around Tread, hugging him tightly, and enjoyed the fact that her mother was back, even it wasn't ever going to be exactly the same.

After a few moments, Tread looked down at her, a smile playing behind his eyes.

"What?" Lilly demanded. "What is so funny?"

"You know that now your parents are going to be able to hear your every move. No more sneaking out."

Lilly shoved him playfully. "Now it will just be more challenging. I'm faster. I'm still a sunwalker after all."

Tread laughed. "This is going to be interesting." He rubbed his chin pensively. "What was going on earlier? You couldn't keep that silly grin off your face."

"Silly?"

"It was still beautiful," he recovered quickly.

"Adam and Annie."

He looked at her cluelessly.

"They're together. Or trying to be."

His eyes doubled in size. "No way!"

"It's still new. That's why they didn't want me to mention it. But I'm glad Annie is going with him. Trying to find Phoenix may not be easy. My aunt wasn't sure she wanted to see her brothers again after how she parted with them."

"Well, we'll need to find a new doctor now," Tread noted.

"I think Lex may be able to help us with that." She nudged him playfully with her hip.

"Come on, Jace. It's time to find a more permanent home," Lilly said as she practically had to drag him away from Luke. "Don't worry, you will see plenty of your new friend."

"Do I get to live with you?" he asked.

"Would you like that?"

Honestly, Lilly hadn't even thought of it. She assumed he'd want to live with Tread.

"Yes." He smiled, sliding his small hand in hers.

"Well, I want you to meet someone first, and if you like her too, then I think that can be arranged."

She took him back to her apartment. Dylan, Elaine, and Tread were all sitting around the kitchen table chatting as they entered.

"Well this handsome young man must be Jace," Elaine said, greeting him warmly.

"Are you Lilly's mother?" he asked.

"Yes, I am."

He nodded. "I've never had a mother. Luke has a mom and a dad."

"I'm sorry," Elaine said.

The boy shrugged. "It's okay. I didn't used to have one, but I found one now. Lilly's going to be my mother."

It warmed her heart to hear the young sunwalker's desire. She had never thought of having children, since she knew it wasn't possible. Lilly had never thought it would be something she missed. But watching Lex and Luke over the past few months had made her wonder.

"Are you sure you want to stay here with me forever?"

He smiled a wide grin. "You've loved me more than Koyt ever did. I never want to leave."

"Well, what about Tread?" Lilly asked.

"He can't be my mom," Jace laughed. "Tread's going to be my dad. Then I'll have a family just like Luke. It will be a forever family, right?"

Tread stood up and knelt down beside Jace. "We'd love to be your forever family."

It hadn't been an easy journey to get to this point in Lilly's life. She had suffered loss, pain, and heartache. Plans had gone awry and life had thrown its share of curveballs her way. But sitting here now at the kitchen table, knowing Lex was going to live, and being encircled with her mother, father, Tread, and Jace, she couldn't imagine anything better.

Epilogue

ONE YEAR LATER

The world had changed so much in the past twelve months. Big eighteen-wheeler trucks were back on the road making deliveries in between cities. Even a few commercial flights had just began leaving out of D.C and a few other major cities.

The Vampire Registration Act had passed three months ago. Basically, it assigned every vampire that registered a social security number. Anyone who wanted to work could work, and vampires would be allowed to vote and run for office starting six months after.

Sam was appointed as the first vampire senator and Alex and Bear had joined the VAS which had now simply been merged into the FBI. They were on a special task team that hunted the few rogue vampires that didn't want to abide by the new laws.

Vampire resistance had been relatively low. Most had welcomed the chance to step out from the shadows, especially now that special pathways and windows were being installed in all the new cities. Being able to see sunlight again without the fear of death was a huge incentive to most nightwalkers.

It took Lilly some time to convince Tread that he needed to register too. He didn't like the thought that they would start tracking him in a sense. But she reminded him that it was the same process all humans went through, only it began at birth for them.

Laws were being made, and cities were hesitantly getting used to seeing vampires at night and even inside some buildings during the daylight hours. Most cities did not have the money to put a dome over their entire municipality. But Lilly had connections in the government and as a thank you for their part in stopping Koyt and his army, Ryan had gifted Spero a special dome made out of the same material as the pathways. This would allow everyone, human and vampire alike, the same freedom to walk through the city at will.

The hope was that one day all cities would have this technology. It was a gift that Lilly felt everyone had the right to. However, the cost was high and it would still be a long while until all the cities across the country had access to them. Hopefully even across the globe.

"Are you sure this has been tested?" Elaine asked hesitantly as Lilly opened the door to their apartment complex widely.

"Yes," Lilly insisted for the hundredth time. "Annie stuck her hand out and when it didn't disappear, she went out in the city. She has already been running around everywhere, enjoying the sunlight. We had double the glass installed just as an added precaution," she added, rolling her eyes. "Now come on!" She grabbed her mother's hand and pulled her outside.

Elaine froze for a moment, then stretched her arm out, letting the light touch her skin. "This is amazing. Even better than the synthetic blood that Lex's dad came up with." Her mother twirled around in the sunlight, her pink dress poofing out as she spun.

"I told you." Lilly beamed.

Lex's dad had really come through with his synthetic blood invention. It wasn't quite as tasty as real human blood, but it kept her just as strong. It was now available in every store. It was helping the humans come together faster with the vampires. Donating blood wasn't a favorite of any of the humans here in Spero and they were thrilled when they no longer had to give blood. Lilly imagined that humans everywhere probably felt the same way. Luckily most had never had it forced upon them.

Lex was doing fantastic. She was back to her old self and she and Ethan had just gotten the okay to start a family. Luke was hoping for a sister.

Lex's parents had visited weekly the first month, but their daughter had soon convinced them to move here. Now Dr. Eric Crews had taken over for Adam as the resident doctor.

"You look pensive," Tread commented.

"I just can't believe it. Everything we hoped for. I keep thinking I should pinch myself so that I know this is real…Ouch!" She turned and shoved him, rubbing her arm. "I meant metaphorically."

"Can I pinch you too?" Jace asked, grinning ear to ear.

"No, pinch your father," Lilly said.

Jace had been the surprise that Lilly never knew she needed. He called them mom and dad now and kept pushing them to get married. He was ready for them to live all under the same roof. And Elaine had made it clear that wouldn't happen until Tread put a ring on her daughter's finger.

School was Jace's new favorite activity. He had been behind when he started, but soaked up everything like a sponge. He was now way ahead of the class and read everything he could get his hands on.

Luke waved from off in the distance and Jace ran off to play.

"Things are pretty much perfect. We'd never have gotten here without your stubborn determination." Tread winked.

The sun was shining, the sky was blue, and now all of Lilly's friends could enjoy the world as she did.

"I'll take that as a compliment," she said as she elbowed him playfully. "Of course, it wasn't without loss. Too many friends paid dearly for this," she added mournfully.

"It seems history really does repeat itself. Everything worth having requires sacrifice." Tread looked out somberly over the city. "I wish Red could have seen this. He'd have been proud of what we accomplished. When I told him of your crazy notions," he cocked his eyebrow up and winked, "he believed you could do it. Even before meeting you. Anyone who could survive that long living with humans had to be incredible."

"If it weren't for Red's bravery and sacrifice, none of this would have happened. He was the incredible one." Lilly wrapped her arms around Tread and hugged him. "I'm happy they added his name to the memorial of all the fallen. We lost too many."

"We did," he agreed, kissing the top of her head. "I am glad you suggested it, especially remembering those senators that lost their lives in Arkansas. You never let anyone be forgotten. I am sure their families appreciated that."

She looked up as footsteps approached. Franny was headed toward her, an envelope in hand.

"Mail came, and there was something for you," Franny said, waving the letter in her hand.

"From Ryan?" Lilly guessed. Although he normally called now, he was an old soul and still liked to correspond the old-fashioned way. It reminded him of how they had gotten so far.

Franny shook her head. "No, not today."

Lilly took the letter and turned it over. It was her uncle's handwriting scribbled across the front of the envelope. She had almost given up hope that he would write. It had been a year and she hadn't heard a word.

Careful not to rip the contents, Lilly tore open the top of the letter and slid out the note.

Lilly,

I'm sorry it took me so long to write. It has taken me longer than I imagined to track down Phoenix. I just kept thinking the next stop I'd find her and then I'd touch base with you. I don't know what I would have done without Annie. Thank you for insisting that someone accompany me and for not giving away my secret.

I appreciate you for encouraging me. Falling in love with another species is not anything I would have ever imagined. Hearing Dylan's screams during his transition gave me pause to think if a relationship with a vampire could ever go anywhere. And although his cries still haunt me, they are not enough to deter me from trying to have my eternity with her.

If things don't go the way we hope, don't blame Annie. She's family. Please treat her as such. If left up to her, she would keep me human, knowing for certain I would be safe, and watch me grow old. But I can't accept a small handful of years knowing I could have had more. I love you so much sweetheart. You brought me more joy than you can possibly imagine. Watching you grow up, family movie nights, reading to you before bed…I treasure every second. My only regret is having wasted the first five years of your life without you.

If all goes according to plan, we will be joining you soon. I have convinced Phoenix and Jimmy to accompany us. She's not sure what to think of her new vampire family after living so many years on her own, but she wants to try. Give Elaine and Dylan my love. I'm proud of you, kiddo. Never forget that. You did the impossible. Tread—yes, I know you'll read this too—take good care of our girl.

Love always,
Uncle Adam

Adam and Annie. A smile formed on her lips and she passed the letter to Tread who had been standing silently at her side, giving her space.

The transition wouldn't be an easy one, but her uncle would survive it. If her father could make it through, even with all his vampire trauma, Adam would be fine.

As a young girl, she had worried about the day her heart would stop beating. Her mother had told her she would live forever. But the moment her heart stopped was always the pivotal moment in her mind. Humans died when their hearts stop beating. That moment in her mind would cement Lilly living alone for all eternity.

It was silly. She knew that even when her heart stopped beating, she would still have decades with her family. But now she didn't have to worry about it.

Lilly's heart had stopped beating about eight months ago. But now there was nothing to fear. Her family would live forever with her. Having her uncle included in that just made her life all the more perfect. It was still a little weird at times, not having blood pumping through her veins or the comforting pitter patter of her heartbeat. But she no longer associated loneliness with the lack of it. All she felt now was ecstatic joy.

Tread read it quickly.

"It still seems surreal. But I'm glad Adam found happiness. He deserves it. Annie too."

"I guess we'll know one way or another in a few weeks."

"He'll be fine. Adam knows what to expect and is still going to go through with it. I don't know if I would be that brave. Listening to those screams was one of the hardest things I have ever done. I don't know that I would be brave enough to go through it."

"Of course you would be. Lil, there is no one braver in this world. And I doubt there ever will be." He chuckled softly.

Lilly took Tread's hand in hers and looked over Spero. She wondered how long it would take her until she truly believed this life, her life, was real. Blissfully happy was a state she wasn't used to being in. Too long she had spent looking over her shoulder, waiting for the other shoe to drop.

She pulled Tread closer and reveled in the happiness that she had never before let herself even dream of feeling. This was her happily ever after. It had been hard fought and lives were lost in the process. She would honor them by living in this new world that their sacrifices had helped create, and she didn't intend to waste one second of it.

Acknowledgements

Writing a trilogy has been a thrilling adventure. It took an awesome support team to get me here. I have been blessed beyond measure to find people who encourage me yet are not afraid to point out mistakes or question inconsistencies in my story.

So, I just want to shout out to a few key people. Please forgive me if I missed anyone. Thank you Kiora, Dawn, Baranie, Courtney, my mom, and of course my family.

Thank you to my readers for joining my on this incredible journey. Ending this saga, I was really torn. Hopefully you were pleased with the ending. However, because I was so torn as to how to finish up this trilogy, I wrote an alternate ending. So if you really hoped for a different finish, you can read it on my blog, authorstsanchez.blogspot.com. If you liked the ending, just steer clear of that particular section.

As always, please don't forget to go online and review my book. It means so much to authors and only takes a minute or two.

Thanks again for letting me share Tread and Lilly's adventure with you.

I love to hear from readers. Drop me a line at authorstsanchez@hotmail.com.

For news about my current projects and other books, be sure to

check out my blog: www.authorstsanchez.blogspot.com

About the Author

Sarah Sanchez has always been a fantasy fan. There are no limits to fantasy beyond one's own imagination. She was born and raised in Texas, where she continues to live with her husband, Armando, three kids, a cat, and a dog. When she's not coming up with her next story idea, she loves baking, spending time outdoors and trying out new restaurants. She is also a huge movie buff and enjoys anything from Harry Potter to Pride and Prejudice. Be sure to check out her other series, The Keeper Archives. Book 1, The Portal Keeper is now available.

Follow me on Twitter @authorstsanchez

Instagram@thekeeperarchives